Operation find a ~~JOB~~ GUY

Roadtrip Romance • Book Three

AMY R. ANGUISH

Scrivenings
PRESS
Quench your thirst for story.
www.ScriveningsPress.com

Published by Scrivenings Press LLC
15 Lucky Lane
Morrilton, Arkansas 72110
https://ScriveningsPress.com

Printed in the United States of America

Paperback ISBN 978-1-64917-299-0

eBook ISBN 978-1-64917-300-3

Editors: Shannon Vannatter and Linda Fulkerson

Cover by Linda Fulkerson, bookmarketinggraphics.com

For my brother Phillip McDoniel, who was one of the reasons I got to experience Colorado in the first place, who has always been fun to hang out with, and who takes amazing pictures of my children for me. I couldn't ask for a better brother.

1

"**B**ut where are the mountains?"

Skye Jones readjusted her sunglasses as her little red convertible flew past the Colorado state line sign. After hours upon hours of seeing the same undulating Kansas fields—not all that different from the hours of Missouri—Skye had looked forward to some elevation. But this scenery was just more of the same—and that reminded her too much of adulthood.

Actually, Missouri had more hills than she saw here. Mountains that tall should be visible even this far away, right? The last time she'd visited Rain, she'd flown, so she had no accurate comparison, but still ... Hadn't she learned something in a geography class long ago about the Rockies being some of the tallest in the United States?

The GPS said she had only about three-and-a half-hours to go. Surely something should appear by now. Skye blew out a breath and pushed the gas pedal just a bit farther. She'd never been given an ETA she wasn't tempted to beat. Besides, she'd left St. Louis at 5:30 that morning—a time no person on earth should have to be awake—and she was ready to be there already.

At least by rising that early, she'd been able to avoid her father. No need to listen to him tell her one more time, 'This is only going to help you temporarily, Skye. I'm serious. If you don't have a full-time job by the end of the summer, that car you love so much is mine.'

"Don't worry, baby." Skye patted her dashboard. "We'll figure something out."

If Rain hadn't offered this compromise, she might be more worried. But helping with Rain's wedding-planning business would buy Skye a few months. Allow her to come up with some miracle to keep her car. *Time to get there already.*

"Get ready, Rain. I'm headed your way." She cranked up the volume on the radio and sang along as the windmills waved from the fields on both sides of the road.

A couple of hours later, Skye found the mountains. The closer to Denver she drove, the higher the peaks reached, the very tops of them still white. Majestic. Denver nestled at the base of the Rockies, and almost distracted her from paying attention to the traffic and signs pointing her toward her final destination.

The view winding up to Boulder proved her sister wasn't completely crazy to have followed Jeremiah out here. Stunning. Sure, she'd been here before, but driving gave her a whole new perspective.

The college town of Boulder was nice. Busy streets, full of organic-loving stores and big-brand names. She huffed as she stopped at yet another red light. Why were there still so many cars out at 6:30 in the evening? Shouldn't most of these people be home by now?

She cut into the right-turn lane on the next block. A bang came from the back of her car, followed by a yell. Her gaze jerked to the rearview mirror. What in the world?

A guy stood on the side of the road, legs planted around his bicycle, shaking a fist her way. Where had he come from, and why was he in the road in the first place? His blue eyes shot sparks her way as if it were her fault she'd almost hit him.

She rolled her eyes and maneuvered through a few more intersections before she finally found her sister's store front. *HEA.* The stylized letters in the logo looked cheerful and promising ... as if happily ever-afters actually existed. It was the *ever* part that always made Skye cringe.

"Guess who!" She sang out as she pushed through the glass door and set some bells jangling.

Rain stepped out from behind a counter and opened her arms. "I wasn't expecting you yet! You must have left at a ridiculous time to get here now."

Skye readily stepped into her sister's hug. "I did. And I'm starved. When can we go eat?"

"Same old Skye, I see." Rain shook her head as she stepped back. "Sorry, Sis. But I can't leave until after my last appointment. He should be here any moment. A groomsman coming in for a fitting."

"A fitting? You rent tuxes now?"

"No. But I coordinate with several places that do. And it's just easier for everyone to get the measurements to me instead of hoping they find the right shop and making sure the tailor knows which event it's for so they get the right color pants ..." Rain waved a hand in the air. "You get the idea."

"Not really, but okay." Skye shrugged and brushed some

hair over her shoulder. "Got anything to hold me over? I really am hungry. I mean, it's getting close to seven."

"Six." Rain pointed at a clock. "You're on Mountain time now."

Skye slumped. "Ugh. I'm going to waste away before I eat anything. I may be in Mountain time, but my stomach is definitely still on St. Louis time."

"Come on. I think I have some almonds or granola bars in my drawer." Rain stepped through a curtain to the back of the store area.

"Since when did you get all healthy?" Skye followed.

"It's hard not to be out here." Rain motioned around her as if encompassing the whole town. "This town is big on being healthy."

"I guess that explains the weirdo on the bike earlier. He got mad at me for driving in the same lane he was trying to ride in." Skye huffed. "As if bikes are supposed to be on the road instead of cars."

"If he was in a bike lane, he had the right of way." Rain tossed her a fruit-and-cereal bar.

"Bike lanes? Aren't those supposed to be over on the shoulders?"

"And sometimes they're combined with other lanes. A lot of people around here like to ride bicycles to work or the store. Get their exercise. During the spring and fall, the weather's gorgeous. The winter, not so much."

"I guess. But he still should've paid more attention. I mean, it was a turn lane for cars."

"Yeah. That's usually where the bike lanes and driving lanes crisscross and overlap."

"You mean I wasn't supposed to drive in the turn lane? Then why have it?" Skye took a big bite out of the bar despite its lack of appeal.

"You can still drive in a turn lane. You just need to pay attention and make sure you don't cut in front of any cyclists." The bell out front drew Rain's attention. "That must be the last groomsman of the day. We'll head back to my place after this, and I'll feed you something real."

"No tofu." Skye pointed at her sister with the last bite of the bar.

"No tofu." Rain held her hands up as she backed through the curtain separating her office from the front part of the store.

Rain's voice mingled with that of a man. He sounded young and maybe a bit breathless. The curtain blocked more sound than Skye would've guessed, but she thought she heard something about a bicycle. The temptation was too great. What were the odds someone would come in from riding a bike right after Rain had said lots of people used that method of transportation?

A sliver of a gap in the curtains afforded her a peek without being seen. Maybe six inches taller than Rain—head of thick dark hair, button-down shirt with the sleeves rolled up, nice slacks. Skye frowned. He looked familiar.

Rain motioned toward another area, and he followed her. Skye sucked in a breath and quickly ducked out of sight. Not just any guy who rode a bike—the one who shook his fist at her earlier.

And much more handsome without a scowl on his face.

"Better just stay back here." She flopped into Rain's chair and surveyed the tidy space.

Never before were the differences between her and Rain more noticeable than here. Where Skye never knew where things were, Rain obviously had a place for everything and had everything in its place. Skye's fingers twitched to move her sister's pens to the other side of the desk just to see if she'd notice.

But Rain was giving her an out for a few months. A cushion of grace to keep her father from stealing her car away.

Her car!

Had the cyclist seen it in the parking lot? Did he know she was hiding back here? Would he rat her out to her sister?

Ridiculous.

He had no idea who she was. Surely there were other red sports cars in Boulder, Colorado. Though the odds seemed stacked against her right now.

Ring.

Rain rushed through the curtain, shot a dirty look at Skye sitting in her seat, and motioned Skye toward the shop floor. "Can you go man the front counter while I take this call, please?"

"But I don't know—"

Rain didn't leave her another moment to make excuses but grabbed the handset and answered with a professional, "Happily Ever After event planning. How can I make your dreams come true?"

If Skye had to say that all summer, she might be more motivated to find another job. Ick. She pushed through the barrier and positioned herself on the stool behind the counter. Surely no one would walk in at five 'til six in the evening anyway. Nothing to worry about.

A door down the hallway opened and footsteps sounded on the hardwood floors. Skye spun around just as a man walked out, a bicycle helmet under his arm. He froze the same moment she did.

There went those odds again. Good thing she wasn't a betting girl.

Maybe he didn't get a good glance at her in the car earlier and was just surprised to see someone other than Rain. Time to play it cool. She flipped a strand of hair over her back and shot him a smile.

Benjamin Smith was many things, but easily shaken was not one of them. Until today. Now this blonde woman had caught him off guard twice—almost maiming him the first time.

"Is Rain still around?" He glanced toward the room where he'd last seen the wedding planner.

"She's in the office for a moment, but she'll be back out after she wraps up a phone call." There went that bright smile again. It probably had lesser men melting. Who was he kidding? It flipped his stomach like a pancake.

"I don't know if she needed anything else or not." He shifted his weight. "Didn't want to leave before making sure."

"No worries. Like I said. She'll be back out in a minute." The blonde tapped her fingers on the counter.

"Do you work here?"

"For now."

Was she about to get fired? What did 'For now' mean? Why not just 'Yes?' "Um ..."

"Rain's my sister. I'm helping her out this summer."

Now that she said it, he could see a few similarities although Rain's hair was a darker shade than this girl's. And their attitudes came across completely different. If Rain had acted this nonchalant, she wouldn't be the wedding planner for the whole church. And he wouldn't have been impressed enough to pass her name on to his cousin Chet. Now he was in two weddings Rain was planning.

And he didn't trust this girl to help with any of it. "Just for the summer?"

"That's the plan for now." She gave a shrug. "Not sure what I'll do after that."

"Hey. Sorry that took so long." Rain breezed through the curtain and Benjamin breathed a sigh of relief. "Okay, Benjamin, are we all set?"

"I hope so. It's been a rough day." He ran his fingers through his hair and stepped closer to the counter, now that Rain was back in charge.

"I'm sorry you had a rough day. Let's just glance through the checklist and make sure I have everything I need." Rain's finger ran down the printed sheet in front of her. "I have the measurements. We've chatted before about all the things you'll be responsible for as best man in Chet's wedding."

"Responsible for?" The sister peeked over Rain's shoulder. "Best men just stand up front and hand over the ring, right?"

"If you're helping this summer, you might want to study up on wedding etiquette a bit more." Benjamin knocked on the countertop in front of her. "There are a few other expectations. The good news is, I'm just a regular groomsman in my sister's wedding."

"You're in two weddings?" Her voice held an offensive tint of incredulity.

"Yes. Don't you have friends who get married?"

"I have friends who were supposed to get married. But they called it off for some reason." She batted a hand in the air. "Probably better that way anyway."

Rain didn't look at all pleased.

"Skye, why don't you go back and wait in the office again? I'll start your official training tomorrow." Rain pointed toward the curtains.

Skye opened her mouth as if to object, but then closed it again and pinched her lips together.

"Might want to train her in how to drive in a town with bicycle lanes." Benjamin pitched his voice just loud enough for her to hear it across the room.

"That was *you*!" Rain's eyes widened. "I am so sorry! She didn't actually hit you, did she?"

A squeak of protest came from Skye's direction.

"No. She missed me by a few inches. Because *I* paid attention to my surroundings."

Another squawk.

"Did we go over everything we needed to? If not, we can do it over the phone another time, right?" Benjamin glanced at his watch and noticed several missed messages. Never a moment off.

"Sure. Sorry to keep you so late. Go on, and I'll let you know if there's anything else I need from you."

"Thanks, Rain." He settled his helmet on his head and started toward the door. As he stepped out into the evening air, he glanced over his shoulder one more time and caught Skye peeking at him through the curtain. She quickly disappeared, and he made his escape.

Rain, he trusted, but that sister ... he wasn't sure about her. What was Rain thinking, hiring her for the summer? Sure, family helps out family. But there had to be a line somewhere.

Oh, well. Not his problem. His problems came in the form of a couple bosses who didn't think the workday ever ended. But just a few more years and he could move beyond the peon level.

Until then, he'd continue to pay his dues, working for one of the elite law firms in Boulder. And helping Chet and Amelia bring about their happily ever afters. His own would have to wait until he was more settled.

Which was okay. Because he hadn't found anyone he'd want to spend forever with yet.

So why did the thought of long blonde hair pop into his head as he contemplated that thought?

2

All things considered, Benjamin probably could've handled this errand with a phone call. That being said, he found himself standing in front of Happily Ever After on Friday afternoon anyway. Might as well go on in.

As soon as he stepped in the door, the woman who hadn't been far from his mind the last four days looked up from her perch behind the counter. If she held any ill will from their last interaction, she gave no indication. Instead, she straightened and flashed him a smile.

"How can I help you today?"

"My sister asked me to touch base with Rain about something for her wedding next month."

"Rain is meeting with a bride right now, but she'll be down soon. Or I can give her a message."

He leaned against his side of the counter. "I can wait."

"Suit yourself." Skye returned her attention to the magazine she'd been flipping through, some bridal periodical, full of fluffy dresses and overdone flowers.

"Planning something for your future?" He pointed to the page that held her attention.

"Doing homework." Skye turned to the next gown.

"I had no idea bridal magazines counted as homework. Will there be a test?" He kept his voice light, hoping to draw back out her feisty side he'd seen on Monday.

"Knowing my sister, probably. Though I can't figure out why anyone would want to go through all of this. Even if I had an inkling of desire to get married someday—which I don't—I wouldn't want such a production. Eloping sounds more my style."

Who was this girl? Had he ever met one who willingly suggested elopement instead of a regular wedding? Or who had no dreams of finding a forever relationship?

"You don't want to get married someday?" He tried to come across as nonchalant, but curiosity urged him to ask more questions. "No boy back home keeping the telephone wires hopping with his nightly calls and words of missing you?"

"Oh, no. I don't have relationships. I only have *flirts*."

"Wait. Did you just call yourself a flirt?"

"No, silly. I said I only had FLIRTS." She held a finger up for each letter. "Fun Living in Right This Second."

He mouthed the words as he made sure they really did correspond with each letter.

"No plans for the future? No dreams of settling down?"

"Nah. I'm more of a live-in-the-moment kind of girl. Having plans takes the spontaneity out of life—makes it dull." She turned another page as if everything on it were the dullest thing imaginable.

"That can't be true." The attorney in him was coming out, wanting to plead his case.

"Can't it?" She flipped a strand of the longest, blondest hair over her shoulder and raised a thin eyebrow. "Do you have fun doing whatever it is you do for a living in a suit like that?"

"A suit like this?" He plucked at his lapel. "What's wrong with wearing a suit?"

"It usually comes with a stuffy job to match." She motioned up and down the length of him with a perfectly manicured nail.

"I'm not sure I'd call being an attorney stuffy." He straightened.

Had there ever been such a perplexing and vexing girl in the world? The more she spoke, the more he wanted to dig deeper and find out all the whys of what she said. But her burst of laughter kept him from traveling down the road of investigation.

"Oh, that's rich." She slapped the counter. "A lawyer. Just perfect."

"I consider law my perfect occupation. I mean, I worked hard enough to get where I am today."

"And you'll be working just as hard for the rest of your life." Skye shook her head. "If that doesn't scream *humdrum* and *dull*, I don't know what does."

He probably should have been offended, but he simply found her 'curiouser and curiouser,' as Alice said in Wonderland. How had someone grown up in the same house as Rain Wilkes and turned out so completely different? Rain was fun-loving, too, for sure. But she also found pleasure in accomplishments and hard work.

"Your name is Skye, right?" He buried both hands in his pockets and rocked back on his heels.

"Yes."

"I guess your parents liked the weather, huh?"

That earned him a moment of attention. "Why do you say that?"

"Rain and Skye?" He tilted his head. "Both seem rather weather-y to me."

"Mm. Or simply unique." She blinked. "Forgive me, but I've forgotten your name. Only that it was some old-man one."

He sputtered. "Old man?"

"Dennis or Dwayne or Bob or something that sounds like it should belong to one of those guys who go sit in the fast-food place and drink coffee all morning." Her lips twitched as if she were testing him.

He unclenched his teeth. "It's Benjamin."

"Right. Like I said, an old-man name." And, as if to show how unconcerned she was about it, she picked up another magazine from behind her and opened it.

"If you must know, it was my uncle's name. And my grandfather's."

"So, you're like, the third or something?"

Surely, she wasn't really this dense? It had to be an act, right? Before he could figure it out, Rain walked down the stairs chatting with another lady.

The other customer laughed and shook Rain's hand before heading out the door. Rain turned and beamed a smile at Benjamin.

"I hope I didn't keep you long."

"Just getting to know your sister a bit." He'd let her take that any way she wished. Though he still wasn't sure he'd actually gotten to know the real Skye. Simply the shallow shell she wore as her armor.

Rain glanced Skye's way, lips pursed, before returning her attention to him. "Did we forget something the other day when you were here?"

"No. Actually, Amelia needed me to run by and pick up whatever it is you wanted her to see. She's gone to visit Clark's family for the weekend and wanted to have it Sunday night when they get back."

"Right. Let me go grab it really fast, and I'll be right back."

"Thanks."

And back to the other conversation.

"If I'm going to be working so hard for the rest of my life, how will I ever find time to drink coffee with all the other boring old men?" He crossed his arms over his chest.

"Should've thought of that before you agreed to take the job." Skye smirked.

"What does a girl with a … unique name like Skye plan for her occupation? You said working for your sister was only temporary, right?"

"I haven't decided yet." She leaned back on the stool until her shoulders rested against the wall behind her. "But it'll have to be something that isn't the same every day. I need adventure and excitement and fun."

"And what kind of job would bring all of that?"

"That's the problem." She shrugged. "I can't figure out a job that would."

"Here we go." Rain came out from behind the curtain and handed him a large portfolio of some sort.

"Oof!" He bent his knees as the weight of the thing landed in his arms. "What on earth is this?"

"Everything I've pulled together on flowers, their meanings, and what goes well together. I also have notes about which smell the strongest versus hardly any scent at all. And which more people are allergic to." Rain ticked the items off on her fingers as she listed them.

"Wow." He repositioned it to a better angle. "That's comprehensive."

"I try to think of anything and everything I might be asked. Saves time in the long run. Just let her know I'll need that back later next week." Rain glanced at her phone. "I have another bride who'll need to make the same decisions then."

"I'll put a sticky note on it before I drop it at Mom's."

"Perfect." She glanced over her shoulder at Skye, who continued to ignore—or at least pretend to ignore—what happened right in front of her. "Skye, can you mark that off my to-do list, please?"

Skye raised her eyes, studied her sister a moment, and then lazily picked up a pencil and drew a line through one of the lower items on the piece of paper to her left. "Is that it for today, Rain?"

"Sorry. I just got a message from a groom that he could rearrange his schedule and come in this evening. Looks like you're on your own for dinner tonight."

Skye huffed. "I realize it's an hour earlier here than back home, but you keep really late dinner hours, Rain."

"My business takes a lot of time. And with Jeremiah traveling with the baseball team more this summer, it works out for us. I don't have to worry about getting home to feed him. And he understands it's my busy season." Rain had either forgotten Benjamin still stood there or simply trusted him to not care that this discussion was happening where he could hear it.

"Who knew a job you described as fun would actually just be a lot of work?" Skye propped her chin on her fist.

"It is fun."

"Uh-huh. And so is Boulder, or so you said. But so far, all I've seen is the inside of this office and your house."

Rain cut a glance his way, and suddenly he knew she'd remembered his presence the whole time. "I have an idea."

Benjamin opened his mouth to object, but couldn't actually form the words fast enough.

"Benjamin is a Boulder native. I bet he could show you

around." Rain flashed him a smile. "Unless you had other plans."

He swallowed an argument, and it settled like a lump of gruel in his gut. "No plans. I was actually about to go grab a bite to eat."

If nothing else, this would allow him more time to ask some of the questions that arose from their earlier conversation.

Skye shook her head. "You're kidding, right? You don't just send your sister off with some guy who happens to be in two different weddings you're planning."

"He's not just some guy. I've known Benjamin the whole time I've lived here." Rain waved her hand through the air. "If I didn't trust him, I wouldn't have suggested it."

"It's still not right. I mean, he's obviously only agreeing because you put him on the spot. He has no desire to spend more time with me than neooooary."

Benjamin stepped forward. "Actually—"

But Rain answered Skye before he could finish that statement. "Weren't you the one who coerced two guys into joining your girls' trip earlier this summer? Wasn't that the story I heard?"

Of course, that would come back to bite her. Why had she boasted about including Camden and Ryan on that stupid road trip? Especially considering how that had ruined things for Bree and Nathan.

"What does that have to do with this?" She motioned between herself and Benjamin.

"I'm just saying that if you're willing to go run around with strangers on a road trip a month ago, you should be more than comfortable going to dinner with someone I've known for several years."

Skye opened her mouth, though unsure what other protest to make, but Rain cut her off anyway.

"Besides, if you don't go to dinner with him, you're stuck here until after I'm done with the groom who's coming in about fifteen minutes. Because you rode with me this morning."

And there went the nail into her coffin.

"It's settled, then." Benjamin straightened. "Did you need to do anything else, or are you ready to go?"

As much as she'd love to say she had other tasks to do, there was nothing but looking through more bridal magazines to familiarize herself with the trends. And her eyes had glazed over enough doing that the last half hour, so she couldn't remember half of what she'd seen. Might as well get this over with.

"Let's go." She hopped down and grabbed her purse before turning to her sister. "And I guess if anything happens to me, you can live with the guilt for the rest of your life."

"I'm willing to take my chances." Rain shook her head before shooing them out the door.

There were only a few vehicles in the parking lot as they headed out into the warm evening. Skye took in each make and model before heading toward a sporty black sedan. Benjamin cleared his throat.

She stopped and looked his way. He head-motioned in the opposite direction of where she'd been walking. But all that was on that side of the lot was an antique orange Chevy pickup truck. No. Surely not.

That didn't mesh with a single bit of the mental image she'd settled on since meeting him.

But Benjamin opened the passenger door for her and

waited until she walked over and climbed in. Though it was obviously ancient, it was well cared for. The leather on the bench seat had no tears or stains—had maybe even been refurbished. The dashboard was shiny as if cleaned on a regular basis. She ran her fingers over the material before she could help herself.

"Admiring my ride?"

"This is what you get around in?" She couldn't keep the incredulity out of her voice.

"A bit sturdier than that little red roller skate you drive, isn't she?" He patted the steering wheel and then cranked the engine.

"Roller skate?" Skye huffed. "Rosie is not a roller skate."

"Mm-hmm." He glanced over his shoulder and backed out.

"She's not." The leather she'd admired moments before didn't give much when she slapped her hands on it.

"Agree to disagree." He wove through traffic easily.

"I guess I should just be grateful you weren't on your bike today."

He snorted. "Not after almost getting hit the other day."

She glanced out her window instead of facing him. "I really am sorry about that."

"I shouldn't have brought it up again. If you had to learn that lesson the hard way, at least it was me you learned it on—not some hothead."

"You didn't look very cool-headed when you shook your fist in my rear-view mirror Monday afternoon." Her lips twitched.

"We'll see how cool you stay if you almost get hit by a car someday." One of his perfectly shaped brows rose as he glanced her way.

"Fair enough." She settled back in the seat. "Where are we going?"

"I thought you might enjoy Pearl Street. It's one of the areas Boulder is best known for. Lots of shopping and eateries."

"That sounds fun." The agreeable words escaped before she could stop them. Now she'd done it.

"Speaking of keeping your cool ..." He tossed her a look that had her squirming. "How about you drop the attitude now that no one else is around to impress?"

"The attitude?" Her spine straightened. "I'm sure I don't know what you're talking about."

"The act you put on back at Rain's shop. All that malarkey about never wanting to get married or only wanting to have fun." He circled his hand in the air. "You don't have to show off anymore. I'd much rather get to know the real you."

"Sorry to disappoint, but that is the real me." She crossed her arms over her chest. The neighborhood around them looked familiar, but she couldn't tell if it was because all the residential streets in this town looked similar or if she'd been down this road before.

"I'm not so sure." Benjamin turned again, and this time Skye was sure she'd gone this way during the last few days.

"Are you sure you know where you're going?" She spotted a few garden gnomes she'd seen that morning. "I thought you said we were headed to a place with shops and restaurants."

"We are. But Pearl Street is pedestrian only. So, I thought we'd park up here and walk the few blocks down to it instead of trying to find one of the few parking spots available." He pulled into her sister's driveway.

"This is Rain's house."

"Yes, it is." He drove up the hill and parked behind Skye's car. "She told you we knew each other."

"And just how do you know my sister?"

"We go to church together." He hopped out and headed around the front of the truck.

She wiggled the door handle, but nothing budged. A good yank from him and the door opened, Skye almost tumbling out from the momentum. Benjamin caught her, one arm around her back and a hand at her waist.

"You okay?"

"Your door is tricky, huh?" She willed her heartbeat to slow down. It was just the craziness of almost falling several feet down to the driveway that had her pulse so erratic. Nothing to do with his muscled shoulders under her fingers.

"A truck that's been around sixty-five years will do that."

"I guess so." She planted her feet and straightened.

After she stood on her own again, he slipped his suit coat off and tossed it in the seat before slamming the door. "Ready?"

"As I'll ever be."

3

From the red brick walkway to the trees sending their dappled shadows over the benches underneath, to the colorful storefronts and awnings over tons of shiny windows, Pearl Street surpassed Skye's expectations. People milled around, filling tables outside restaurants, strolling past shops, and sitting anywhere they could find a spot. And on every block, the aroma of something yummy, be it coffee or bread or real food, had Skye's stomach protesting that they hadn't stopped yet.

"What kind of food are you in the mood for?" Benjamin's hand rested on her lower back as he steered them around a couple of women who were window shopping.

"I honestly don't care." She stepped a bit farther from him so he had to remove his hand. "What's good?"

"Everything." He chuckled. "A lot of the places down here are local, and most of them use fresh, in-season ingredients. It's hard to go wrong."

"You don't have a favorite, then?"

"I have several favorites, but I don't mind trying something new."

Was he admitting to being adventurous? Just when she'd thought she had him completely pegged, he threw another stone into her picture, sending ripples through the image until it blurred again. Time to shake him up, then. See if he really was as adventurous as he thought he was.

"Okay. I have an idea."

"Okay." No hint of doubt or uncertainty tinged his voice.

"Next person we see carrying a takeout box—whatever restaurant it's from is where we'll eat." She watched for his reaction.

He rubbed his hands together and scanned the crowd. "Let's do this."

Really?

Of course, now that she'd suggested it, no one carried anything by but shopping bags. She tilted her head to read the words on one dangling from a stroller, but it looked like a coffee shop. Had she come up with a plan that wouldn't work?

"There!" Benjamin tugged her arm and headed toward a couple walking the other way.

No logo showed on the bag, but the contents were obviously take-home containers. Okay. She followed his lead.

"Excuse me." Benjamin waved them down and gave a friendly smile when they turned, looking confused. "Sorry, but we were wondering where you ate dinner tonight."

The woman glanced at the man and gave a shrug.

"Just over there." He pointed back a ways and said a name Skye couldn't understand.

"Thanks so much. It smelled so good, we thought we'd try it." Benjamin turned a cheeky grin to Skye and motioned her back toward the restaurant. "Right this way."

"You know this place?"

"I've heard of it. Some of my coworkers gush about it all the time, but I've never checked it out." He stopped in front of an orange door. "Hope you're in the mood for curry."

Inside, middle-Eastern music mingled with spicy scents and happy chatter. Skye breathed deeply, appreciating the mirrors on the walls that enhanced the candlelit tables and booths. When the hostess asked if they had a preference for seating, Benjamin requested a patio table, though.

Exactly what she'd have chosen if he'd asked.

"Two mango lassi, please." His reply was quick when the server asked what they'd like to drink.

"Did you just order for me?" Skye frowned at him over her menu.

"Sorry. It's my favorite drink when I eat Indian food, so I didn't even think about the fact that you might want something different."

"What is it, exactly?"

"It's this mango yogurt drink they have. Super creamy and nice. Especially nice when the heat of the curry hits."

"I would never have picked you for a guy who liked Indian food."

"Or someone who drives a fifty-seven Chevy. Or someone who would run up to a stranger just to ask what they'd eaten for dinner." He didn't even look up from his menu as he stated all her shattered preconceived notions from this evening.

Rather than give him the satisfaction of answering, she studied the menu, reading the descriptions of each dish. "I have no idea what some of these things are."

"I haven't eaten here before, but at the other places I've eaten, I've figured out a few things I like. I would offer to order for you, but you didn't seem to appreciate it the last time." He winked.

She couldn't keep the small laugh from escaping. "I just wasn't expecting it."

"Here's a sampler platter. And it's probably enough food to share, if you want. Then, if we have room, we can grab some ice cream before heading back to Rain's house."

"I always have room for ice cream." Her finger traced the different dishes in the sampler and then found the longer descriptions to figure out what they were. "Okay. Let's do that."

"Here's your mango lassi. Are you ready to order?" The waitress set two cups of bright orange liquid in front of them.

Benjamin glanced at her with a grin before telling the waitress what they'd decided. "And can we get a basket of naan?"

"Of course."

He handed her their menus and settled back to sip his drink. "Perfect."

Skye wasn't about to let him know this unexpected side of him daunted her. Normally when she dated, she was the one suggesting new things or putting the other person in unusual circumstances. Today he'd turned the tables.

"What made you decide to come work with Rain? You didn't sound enthused about the job."

She scowled for a moment. "It's sort of a compromise for now."

"How's that?"

"My father said I need a job. I didn't have one lined up. He threatened to take my car. Rain offered a position for the summer until I can figure out what I want to do." She traced the curves in the patterned tile on their tabletop. "I hadn't seen Colorado yet, except during a quick family Christmas right after Rain got married, so I decided it would work as well as anything."

"But you don't really like wedding planning."

"Don't get me wrong. I can see where there's a market for it. But I don't understand why. Why focus so much on one day?" She took a drink of her mango thing and enjoyed the tangy creaminess. If he was right about the rest of their dinner, too, she might have to come back here again before she left at summer's end.

"What are you hoping for when looking for a job?"

A sigh escaped, and she leaned back in her wrought-iron chair. "I don't know. Nothing sounds fun to me."

"Fun again, huh?"

"Yes. Fun." She rolled her eyes. "Is there something so bad about wanting to enjoy the job you're stuck in for the rest of your life?"

"Not at all." He took another drink. "That's why I chose law. I love to prove my point, and my mom always told me I should put my argumentativeness to good use. So I took her advice. Now I get paid to argue."

Another giggle escaped. What was wrong with her? Was she really enjoying hanging out with an attorney? Obviously, the thinner air here in Colorado was messing with her head.

"But don't you find the long hours behind a desk tedious? How can you stand to be inside all day long when you're surrounded by all this?" She motioned to the mountains hovering over them. "I'm not sure I could handle it."

The waitress set several dishes in front of them, along with extra plates. "Enjoy."

"Thank you." Benjamin waited until she left again and then offered his hand. "Pray with me?"

She hesitated for a moment before slipping her fingers over his and bowing her head.

One more hurdle overcome. Benjamin hadn't been sure she'd agree to hold hands during the prayer, but her dainty fingers rested on his while he offered a short blessing. He squeezed her hand as he raised his head.

"Let's dig in." He picked up her plate and scooped out a bit of everything.

"What is all this?" She used her fork to poke at the lamb.

"That one is lamb, I think. It's a curry, so it's got a little spice. Same for the chicken. That one is the mango chutney. This is a vegetable samosa. And that is naan, which is a flatbread."

"Okay."

He held his breath while she chewed her first bite. Her lips turned up into a smile more genuine than he'd seen yet, and all the tension he hadn't realized he'd been holding slipped away. Simply finding a meal she enjoyed felt like a huge accomplishment.

Something about this whirlwind of a girl who couldn't seem to find anything to land on made him want to convince her to stay right here. As if he could offer her enough adventure and excitement to overcome whatever else might pull her away. Not if he couldn't find a job she considered 'fun.' To say nothing of her adamant opposition to being in a serious relationship—ever.

The cards were definitely stacked against him. But she was the first girl he'd desired to impress since ninth grade. And that had to mean something.

"So, you like arguing and old trucks and aren't afraid to try new foods." Skye pointed at him with her fork.

"Does all that fit with my 'old-man name'?" He smirked as he took a big bite out of his samosa.

"Make fun all you want, but you know I'm right." She tore off a piece of naan and used it to sop up some of the chutney.

"And the thing about it is, I can't even shorten it. Because Ben sounds more like an old man than Benjamin. And Benji just sounds like a dog or something."

He choked on his drink, the cool liquid burning the inside of his nose.

"Sorry!" She passed him an extra napkin.

"Just wasn't expecting to go from a geezer to a dog like that." He swiped at the tears in his eyes. "I'll be sure to let my mom know how much you appreciate her passing the family name on to me."

"You won't really!" Her head jerked up.

"Of course not." He set the napkin aside and took another drink. "But you have to admit, you're being a bit ridiculous about this. I mean, Benjamin was the youngest of Jacob's sons in the Bible."

"But in the Bible, they had all sorts of names we wouldn't give our kids today." She shook her head. "That doesn't count at all."

Had she said 'our kids' meaning his and hers together or just in general? He wasn't about to ask. Not when her armor was finally slipping a bit.

"I guess I'll get used to it eventually, but you don't hear many *young* guys with that name anymore." She scooped up the last bite of her meal and then sat back with her last chunk of bread.

"You'd have to be around it pretty regularly to get used to it." He raised an eyebrow as he polished off the rest of his own plate.

"You know what I meant." She tossed her bread at him.

"I don't know. I mean, we've only known each other a few days. I probably can't pick up on all the nuances of how you talk." He smirked.

She opened her mouth with a protest he was sure would be a

zinger, but the waitress chose that moment to bring their check. He took care of it, noticing Skye never offered to help pay even if he'd been willing to let her. Did she consider this a date or simply her right as someone who'd admitted to being unemployed?

They stood and made their way back through the restaurant and out into the evening. He wasn't quite ready to take her back to Rain's house yet. Not when they'd made such headway in her letting the real Skye show. Hopefully she wouldn't notice he kept their pace closer to a stroll than a walk.

"So ... ice cream?" She shot him a half-grin.

"You really have room for ice cream after that dinner we just ate?" He patted his own stomach, still full of naan.

"I told you. I always have room for ice cream." She paused outside a boutique with windows full of boho-style clothes.

"You want to go look?"

"I probably shouldn't. But that top is really cute." She pointed to a blouse with flowers all over the upper half.

"I could see something like that on you."

"Honestly, I probably have one similar in my wardrobe back home. But I only brought part of it for now. Crammed in Rain's guest bedroom, I don't have quite as much space as in my father's house."

The way she referred to her dad sounded so formal. He almost asked her about it but held off. Something told him she wasn't ready yet.

"If you'd rather, we could get coffee." He pointed to one of his favorite spots.

"Caffeine and me this late in the day is not a good combination."

"I would've figured you wouldn't care about that. Just give you more time to have fun."

"Here's a little secret about me." She leaned closer, and he held his breath, waiting to see what was about to come out. "I like sleep too much to make that risk worth it."

He exhaled with a laugh. "Got it. How about tea? There's a nice tea place just up ahead."

"Not really a tea girl, either. Never have acquired a taste for it. It's like drinking dirty water." She wrinkled her pert little nose.

"Maybe you just haven't had a good cup yet."

She shook her head. "I think we should just stick to ice cream."

"Right this way." He motioned toward the other side of the road. "There's a place over here that was featured on one of those TV shows about amazing food all over the country."

"Must be good." She followed him through the glass door and took a deep breath.

"Their waffle cones are the best."

"They smell amazing. Got a favorite flavor?" Her eyes scanned the menu board.

"Let's see what's available today. They only do so many flavors each day, so you never know what you'll get to choose from."

"Mm. Blueberry white chocolate chip sounds good."

"Agreed." He pointed to the Daily Specials board. "And we're in luck. It's on the list."

"Okay." She gave a quick nod. "That's what I want. In a waffle cone."

"No crazy way of picking a flavor or asking a person what they just chose or anything else?" He stared at her, waiting to see if she would change her mind.

"Nope. I'm good."

"Okay, then."

They moved forward in the line and placed their orders.

She didn't even glance in the case to see if another flavor caught her eye. Yet another side of Skye he hadn't expected.

At her first big bite, she actually sighed. He couldn't help but grin and watch her enjoying her treat. Her eyes widened when she noticed him.

"You're about to drip."

"What?" He glanced at his cone. "Oh. Thanks."

"Should we eat while we walk? Surely Rain will be home by now."

"All right. But since we're down here anyway, we should walk by the *Mork and Mindy* house on the way."

"The what house?" Her head jerked in his direction.

"The house where they filmed *Mork and Mindy*. You know? The old TV show?"

"Never heard of it." She nibbled the edge of her cone.

"It was this sitcom about an alien who came to earth and ended up living with Mindy, who sort of took care of him and showed him the ropes about living on earth. Had, um, oh, what's his name?" He pounded his palm against his head for a moment. "Robin Williams."

She shrugged. "I guess we can go by there, if it's that important to you."

He chuckled but led the way. Several blocks later, they stood in front of the old Victorian house. Skye tilted her head as she studied it.

"It's pretty."

"I've always thought so."

"Still doesn't trigger any memories of this strange show, though."

"I guess my parents liked to watch reruns more than yours." He finished off his cone and licked his fingers.

"Probably. Nothing but the latest and greatest for my

father." She whipped out her phone and swiped across the screen. "Let's take a selfie since we're here."

"What?"

"Don't you take selfies? You said this was a famous place. Let's document it." She turned to where her back was to the house and held the phone out before glancing over where he remained facing the other way. "Come on."

He turned around and leaned in close.

"Say, 'Random old sitcom house!'" She pushed the sing-songy words through her smile.

"Nanu-Nanu." Benjamin held his hands up like Mork used to as she snapped the picture.

"What was that?"

"It's what Mork used to say."

"If you're the alien, I guess that means I'm the human who has to take care of you?" She glanced both ways down the sidewalk.

"Something like that."

"Um. Which way to Rain's house? I'm a bit turned around."

He chuckled before turning her to their right. "Here we go. Maybe this alien has a better sense of direction."

"Or something." They were fairly quiet on the way back.

Every now and then, she exclaimed over a flower she wasn't familiar with—especially the tall pink ones that looked like giant puff-balls. Toward the end of the walk, she paused a few times to adjust her sandals and rub her heels. He hadn't considered how unused to walking she might be.

"Here we are."

She glanced up the steep driveway and sighed. "Only a giant mountain left to climb before I can get rid of these shoes."

"You've got this." He wove her arm through his. "Come on."

"Thanks for this evening. It was surprisingly fun."

"Glad I could brighten your humdrum life." He tugged her as she slowed near the top. "Almost there."

"You must think I'm some spoiled little rich girl."

"Nah." He let go as she touched the handle of the back door. "Just someone I find fascinating."

After he climbed in his truck, he glanced over his shoulder and discovered her still watching him. He shot a wink her way before backing up and easing down the driveway. And wondered what other excuses he could find to go to Happily Ever After over the next few weeks. Being in two weddings next month, surely someone needed him to do something there.

4

"Oh, no!" Amelia cried.

Benjamin spun around. What tragedy had happened now? She stood holding that huge portfolio he'd brought home for her.

"What's wrong?"

"I was supposed to have this back to Rain by this evening, but this is Tuesday, and I promised Clark we could go to his business dinner tonight. Didn't she need it back for another bride?" Amelia looked like she'd just killed someone's puppy, certain she'd let Rain down.

"Calm down. My evening is free. I'll run it by for you."

"Really, Bennie? That would be so great." She plopped the anvil-weight notebook in his arms. "You're the best."

He hadn't brought up his sister's nickname for him the other day when Skye suggested alternatives. Somehow it wouldn't be the same if Skye used it. No. She'd have to come up with her own—assuming she stuck around long enough for that.

He accepted the kiss Amelia pressed to his cheek. "That's what brothers and groomsmen are for, right?"

"Sounds good to me!" She flitted out of the room, humming some song she and Clark had picked for their wedding.

He grinned, glanced upward, and whispered, "Thanks for the excuse, God."

Not that he hadn't caught a glimpse of Skye on Sunday during church services. But there had been no chance to talk to her before Mom was ready to leave. And he'd been itching to come up with some reason to spend time with her once again.

The office didn't seem to agree with his desire to get away as early as possible, though. Instead, everything went wrong that morning, from the printer jamming, to the computers being down for half an hour, to one of the aides being out with a summer cold. Benjamin planted himself in his chair and helped pick up the slack since he was the junior attorney.

Then three different documents needed to be prepared and signed before five. And he wasn't told until a quarter to four. Between him and another aide, they got it done. He rushed into the conference room, where one of the senior attorneys and the clients waited.

But the clients asked for about fifteen changes before they would sign anything. He groaned as he sat back at his computer at 4:45 and got back to work. So much for getting out of here on time.

Finally, at 5:40, he shut things down and headed out into the evening. Good thing Rain didn't lock her doors until six or later most days. Not that he didn't know where she lived. He pulled into the parking lot and grinned at a certain red convertible sitting there.

"Thanks again, God."

He scooped up the portfolio and entered the building, a bit

of a bounce in his steps. Skye looked up from her spot at the counter and returned his smile. And the difference in how that felt compared to the last time, when she'd pretended to look at a magazine, filled his insides with warmth.

"What brings you by today? In another wedding?" Her teasing was comfort to his ears after the long day.

"Amelia couldn't get by today and wanted to return this to Rain as soon as possible." He set the heavy notebook on the counter.

"Thank you very much." Skye moved it back behind the counter. "Rain was actually asking about it earlier, so I know she'll be glad to have it back."

"I was glad to play delivery boy."

"Oh, yeah?" Skye leaned forward, her eyes almost twinkling with the joy behind them.

"Yeah. I had something I wanted to ask you." He leaned forward on his side.

"Let me guess." She tapped a manicured nail against her chin. "You want to know what I had for dinner last night so you can know where to go today."

The chuckle that burst from his insides released the rest of the stress that had settled there during work. "Not exactly. I was wondering if you were free anytime on Saturday."

"Um." Skye frowned. "Why do I feel like I'm not free on Saturday?"

"Because you have to help me with a wedding that evening." Rain's voice carried through the curtain.

"Eavesdropper!" Skye called in her sister's direction.

"It's not like you didn't know I was here and could hear everything." Rain poked her head out.

"I thought you were still on the phone call that came in a bit ago."

"Nope."

Benjamin decided to break up the fight before it could happen. "What time will you need Skye to help you? Could I steal her away for the morning?"

Rain glanced back and forth between the two of them for a moment before nodding. "I need her no later than two. I can handle everything until then."

"Done. I'll pick her up from your place around nine-thirty." He rapped his knuckles on the countertop.

"Oh, you will, will you?" Skye straightened. "I don't get a say at all, huh?"

Oops. "Sorry. I guess I just assumed you'd want to come— since you didn't sound happy when you remembered you were busy that day."

"I don't know. Where are we going?"

"One of the best places in Boulder." And he wasn't going to tell her until they got there.

She narrowed her eyes. "And that's supposed to tempt me?"

"Let's just say that I think this place will challenge something you said the other night. Maybe make you change your mind."

"I hope it's something that will make her change her mind about finding a job." Rain threw over her shoulder as she headed back into her office.

Skye's glare might've been more effective if her sister had seen it. Or not. Amelia never paid attention to any glares Benjamin threw her way, either.

"My plan has nothing to do with a job, for the record. I simply thought to give you a fun, new experience and show you one of my favorite places in the area." He rested his arms against the countertop and waited, ignoring the tension running through his body again. How had this girl come to mean enough in his life that he was desperate to spend as much time with her as possible?

"All right. Might as well. Otherwise, I'll probably just be put to work early."

"Heaven forbid!" Rain's voice carried through the curtain again.

"Trouble in paradise?" Benjamin lowered his voice.

"Just a busy day. Evidently, I didn't get a few things done the way she thought I should, so she ended up doing them again. It's not my fault her standards are too high for her own good." Skye's whisper was practically a hiss.

"Sounds a lot like my day." He squeezed her fingers. "Hang in there. Rain has a reason for doing things to a certain standard. And it's gained her quite a bit of business in the two years since she opened. Do it her way for now, and when you figure out what kind of business you want to have, you can do things your way."

"Ew. I don't think I'd want the pressure of running a business."

"You might surprise yourself. Keep thinking about it, and I'm sure the perfect job will show up." He stepped back before he was tempted to grab her hand again. "I'll see you Saturday."

"All right. See you then." One corner of her mouth curved up. "Unless you find yet another reason to come by here."

"You just never can tell." He gave a shrug and headed out the doorway, his lips pursing into a whistle as he made his way back to the truck.

"What exactly was all that about?" Rain popped back out of the office, her purse over her shoulder.

"What?" Skye gathered her own things. "I'm guessing you're ready to go."

"I am ready to go, but I want to know what's going on between you and Benjamin Smith."

"As far as I know, we're having fun together." Skye hit the button on the phone to roll it to the after-hours message.

"And that's it? Does he know it's just fun?" Rain waited at the door, keys in hand.

"Well, I told him straight out the other day that I didn't do serious relationships. So I would assume so." Skye frowned as she walked past her sister and waited for her to lock the door.

"I've just never seen him act like that around a girl before. Makes me nervous." Rain slid into the passenger side of Skye's car.

"Do you want me to not go?" Skye pushed down a big lump of disappointment at that thought. She was only sad that she wouldn't get to see whatever fun place Benjamin wanted to show her—it had nothing to do with spending time with him.

Rain let out a big sigh. "No. I know you'll have fun wherever it is he's taking you. I just want to make sure you're not leading him on."

"I'm not trying to, if it makes you feel better." Skye easily maneuvered back to Rain's house, although the driveway still made her nervous. These homes built into the side of a hill where the first story was down near the street and the middle level was even with the top of the driveway were strange.

"Maybe just find a way to drop a reminder that you don't do serious relationships or something." Rain paused. "I mean. Unless you want to have a serious relationship with him. In which case, I approve."

Skye shook her head and climbed out. "You know me better than that. I don't want to settle down with one person or stay in one place. Not when there are so many places left to explore."

"Yeah, well, if you don't get a job by the end of the summer, it's going to be awfully hard for you to explore all those places on foot." Rain shot her a look as they entered the house. "Plus, traveling costs money."

"Thanks, oh glum one." Skye propped her hands on her hips as Rain set her purse down and opened the refrigerator.

"Look, you know I've got your back. Otherwise, you wouldn't even be here right now. I would've just let you fend for yourself in arguing with Dad."

Rain tugged a loaf of bread out and then dove back in to rummage in the deli drawer. "But it worked out for both of us for you to come help. This is my busiest summer since starting Happily Ever After, and I appreciate you being willing to step in. That being said, things slow down in the fall, and I probably won't have enough business to keep someone else on staff full-time. And then what will you do?"

"I haven't thought that far ahead, but I'll figure it out." Skye accepted the sandwich makings from her sister and set them on the counter. "And I do appreciate you letting me come out here. I just didn't expect you to be preaching the same sermon as our father for my whole stay."

"I'm not trying to preach to you. I'm just worried about you. It's my prerogative as a sister to want you to be taken care of." Rain stopped and released a big breath before grabbing a couple plates. "And, to get back to where this conversation started, I don't want to see my friend hurt."

"And I don't want him to be hurt, so you don't have to worry about it." Skye spread some mayo on her bread. "But where is all this coming from? I mean, you're the one who sent us out together to get dinner the other day."

"Because I knew you were starving and that he'd be a good

one to show you around. I guess I didn't expect the flirting I picked up on today."

"You know I have FLIRTS." Skye rolled her eyes and snagged a piece of Swiss cheese.

"Not your stupid acronym to get away with never doing anything serious or worthwhile." Rain whipped her hand through the air as if to brush the very idea aside. "Flirting like what men and women do when they like each other and want to see where something might lead."

"I think you're reading too much into the whole situation." Skye pressed her other piece of bread to the top of her ham sandwich and took a bite. "Relax."

"I don't have time to relax." Rain took a bite of her own sandwich and chewed a few minutes. "I have five weddings scheduled over the next four weeks."

"Now, see?" Skye grabbed a bottle of water and took a sip. "You're just reinforcing my opposition to finding a full-time job."

Rain shook her head. "Someday, dear sister of mine, you're going to find a reason to stay put for a while and quit flirting with life."

"I hope I never quit flirting. Even if I do end up married, like you think I will." Skye grabbed a carrot and tapped it against her chin. "It's too much fun."

"I mean, Jer and I still flirt. So, I get that." Rain winked as Skye grimaced. "But I'm talking about more than just making little flirty comments and faces with some guy. I'm talking about your whole life. It's right here ahead of you, full of possibilities, just waiting for you to pay attention long enough."

"I don't know what you're talking about. I pay attention to my life."

"Only until something you don't like happens."

"Look, I agreed to come and work with you this summer. I

did not agree to nightly counseling sessions or to having you continue your self-appointed role of my mother. Mom's been gone for nine years. I didn't need you to take her place when she died, and I don't need that now. I'd much rather keep you as just my sister."

"I'll always be your sister." Rain rested a hand on Skye's shoulder. "But that doesn't mean I can't mother a bit."

Skye swallowed a lump of emotion. This summer wasn't supposed to be so full of emotions and intensity. She'd rather consider it her last hurrah before giving in to the reality of life after college and all that entailed.

"Maybe you need to expand your family so you can have someone else to mother." Skye waggled her eyebrows.

"Maybe I'm working on that." Rain smirked and then meandered out of the room, leaving Skye standing there, mouth agape.

Well, that was unexpected.

And a bit surreal. Rain as a mother. Sure, her getting married and moving out here with Jeremiah three years before had proven she was an adult. And starting and rocking her own business had reinforced it. But to be responsible for another person ...

Wow.

Skye swallowed her last bite of dinner and put her plate in the dishwasher. And that would make her Auntie Skye. Well, no doubt about it. She'd be the most fun auntie the world had ever seen.

But a sense of responsibility settled deep inside her. A niece or nephew would be looking up to her. Did she like what they would see?

All the joy of looking forward to another outing with Benjamin faded a bit with the reality.

5

"What's a person supposed to wear when she doesn't know where she's going?" Skye rushed up the stairs and cornered Rain where she sorted through various wedding decorations in the living room. "How should I dress?"

Rain raised her eyes without moving her head, her eyebrows arched. "Does it look like I have time to worry about your little outing this morning?

"My bride suddenly decided—the morning of her wedding, no less—that she couldn't possibly have any baby's breath in her corsages or bouquets. So I have to go through each corsage and pick out the tiny little white flowers. And this girl has ten groomsmen plus ushers, mother-of-the-bride, father-of-the-bride, and various other people who just had to have a corsage or boutonniere."

Skye hesitated, opening her mouth to volunteer her help. But a glance at the clock showed only five minutes before Benjamin was supposed to arrive, and she was still in pj's. First she'd get dressed. Then maybe she'd have a few minutes to help.

"Sorry." She dashed back down the stairs and grabbed a pair of capris and a flowy top. A dab of gloss and a quick swipe with the mascara wand, and she was as ready as she could get. Hopefully he wasn't planning on hiking or anything. Her flats wouldn't last long if that were the case. Plus she wasn't sure she'd have time to shower again before helping Rain this afternoon.

The doorbell rang as she made her way back up the stairs—if nothing else, this summer was great for her legs and glutes. Rain was letting Benjamin in as Skye came through the kitchen. He glanced over Rain's shoulder and grinned. Skye's stomach flipped over itself, and she paused. Had she eaten something funny for breakfast?

"You ready?"

"I guess." Skye spun in a circle. "I wasn't sure what to wear since I didn't know exactly what we're doing."

"That'll be perfect."

"Here." Rain pulled a hair band from her wrist. "You're probably going to want this."

Skye frowned as she accepted the black elastic. "Why?"

"Just trust me." Rain smirked and returned to her flowers.

Benjamin just shook his head and opened the door. "After you."

"Should I be nervous?" Skye slid into his truck and then slipped the rubber band over her wrist.

"Nope. This is going to be fun. You'll see." He carefully backed around and then inched down the driveway and headed through Boulder.

"And you said this is one of your favorite places?" Skye kept her eyes alert, trying to guess where they were headed.

"No place like it anywhere I've ever been." They neared the edge of town, and he kept going.

"I thought you said it was in Boulder."

"It's near the city limits." He took a side road. "Just trust me."

"I'm trying."

"I thought you liked to have adventures and try new things."

"I do. I just prefer to know what adventure or new thing I'm about to do." A hint of whininess lined her voice, and she grimaced. The last thing she wanted to sound like was a brat.

A few minutes later, he pulled into a parking lot. Nestled in a valley with the mountains standing guard behind, a large building boasted a sign that read "Celestial Seasonings." She studied the windows and green trim on the eaves. What was this place?

He opened her door and held out a hand to help her down. As if it were the most natural thing in the world, his fingers slipped to her lower back as they walked across the parking lot. He opened the door and the most amazing mixture of aromas hit her all at once. She closed her eyes and took a deep breath.

"That's my favorite part." His whisper pulled her back to reality.

"Where are we?"

"You don't recognize the name?" He pointed to a picture of a bear wearing a night cap. "Celestial Seasonings tea?"

"Tea? I thought we established the other day that I don't like tea." She propped her hands on her hips as she looked around.

"Well, I bet you might see things differently after this morning. They do tours every hour, but while we wait we can sample some of their flavors." His fingers brushed hers as he handed her a small cup of some sort of deep brown liquid.

She wrinkled her nose. "Dirty water?"

"Blueberry tea. Try it."

One of her eyebrows rose while she watched him down his own sample. "Are you seriously pulling my leg right now?"

"Did I steer you wrong at dinner the other night?" A challenging expression of his own settled over his face, and she noticed for the first time that his blue eyes tended more toward grey near the edges.

"I think we discovered dinner the other night by asking someone else where they went."

"But I knew to order the mango lassis." He nudged her hand holding the cup. "Try this. It's seriously like drinking a blueberry."

Resting the cup on her lips one more moment, she shot him a look she hoped read, 'This better be good, or we're leaving,' and then she tilted the liquid into her mouth. And swallowed a bit of her pride along with the tea. The bitter flavor she normally associated with tea was nowhere to be found.

Benjamin didn't even ask if she liked it. Obviously he could tell from whatever expression was on her face. He moved to the next sample station and poured out a bit for each of them. The card said it was Madagascar Vanilla.

It smelled good. She sipped it and discovered the vanilla covered up most of the tea flavor. Okay. Maybe he was on to something after all. Not that she was about to turn British or anything anytime soon.

"I like the teas they make here because a lot of them are caffeine-free. And they use all these natural ingredients." Benjamin handed her a third cup. "But this is one they've only had for a little while. It's a dirty chai."

"Dirty?" She paused with the cup halfway to her mouth.

"It means with coffee mixed in. You like coffee, right?"

"Love coffee."

He nodded to her sample. "See what you think."

This was the best yet. She sent a smile his way. Maybe he

was better at finding adventures than she had first thought. Though she still couldn't figure out how someone could have so much fun doing things like this yet also willingly work a stuffy desk job.

"Looks like they're getting ready to do a tour." He motioned toward a small crowd gathering at the other end of the counter. "Better go join them if we want to get you back to Rain for the wedding."

"They actually let us go back and see where the tea is made?"

"They do." He accepted a small pack of tea bags from the person in charge.

Skye accepted her own and studied the lemons on the front of it. "Why are they giving us tea?"

"It's your ticket. And a small gift you can take home." He tapped her pack. "I like this flavor when I have a cold. It's nice on a sore throat."

"I'll keep that in mind."

"May I have your attention, please?" The man in charge waved his arms over his head until everyone quieted down. "Thank you. We're about to start our tour, but before we can let you go back into the factory, we have a few rules."

Rules. What kind of rules could they possibly have for a factory that made tea? It wasn't nearly as tempting as if this were a candy-making facility.

"Because we're dealing with a food product, when we go through this door, I'm going to give you all our most glamorous accessory to wear for the duration while you're in the actual factory." He held up something blue with some elastic on one side. Several people tittered with amusement, but Skye shrank back in disgust. Was that a hair net?

"We can't have loose hairs floating around the area where tea is manufactured, so we'll need you to cover it up. This is our one requirement for taking the tour." He glanced around the group. "Sir, I'm going to make sure you have one for your beard, too, okay?"

Benjamin rubbed his smooth chin beside her and Skye's lips twitched. She usually preferred a guy with just a bit of scruff about his face, but in this case, a guy was probably happy to have taken the time to remove the whiskers. Besides, she couldn't imagine Benjamin not looking impeccably clean and put together.

"Ready to rock the hair covering?" Benjamin tapped her wrist. "I bet Rain thought that would help keep your hair in the net a bit better.

"So much for looking cute today." Skye finger-combed her hair into a messy bun on top of her head and followed the rest of the crowd through the doors, taking the offered hair net between two fingers. This had to be the most demeaning thing she'd ever done.

"Something tells me you'll still look cute." Benjamin whispered in her ear right before slipping the blue paper hat over his own head.

Skye took a deep breath to settle the churning in her tummy. Had the yogurt from this morning gone bad or something? She stretched the elastic and slipped the thing over her head, poking some loose hairs up underneath it. But she didn't face Benjamin—though why it mattered what he thought of how she looked, she couldn't fathom.

"You've missed a piece here." Benjamin gently took the blonde strand and pushed it underneath Skye's cap. So silky and soft, he almost didn't want to let go.

She glanced up at him, and something flickered through

her blue eyes he couldn't decipher. What was it about this girl that had him itching to find out more, to share new experiences with her, to find out who she really was? He lowered his hand and flashed a smile.

"Have I found my new style?" He fluttered his lashes and patted his own head covering.

"Mm. I'm not sure this is a trend that will catch on anytime soon. Thank goodness!" She reached up and touched her own, as if afraid it might stick there forever.

"Well, I was right anyway." He tugged the front of hers down a bit lower. "You're still cute."

That nose of hers wrinkled up again, but her cheeks also deepened to a rosier shade of pink, and he couldn't help but celebrate the success of his statement.

"Everyone covered and ready to go?" The tour guide got their attention. "Please don't touch anything while we go through here. Remember how you would feel if you knew someone else had been touching food you might eat down the road. And stay within the lines I point out. Otherwise, let's have fun exploring some tea."

Skye rolled her eyes, but she grinned as she moved beside Benjamin into the factory itself. He never got tired of hearing about tea and where it came from, as well as the different varieties. But he wasn't sure what Skye would think. Suddenly this plan didn't seem as smart as it had earlier, when she'd enjoyed their samples.

But her eyes didn't glaze over through the background part, and then they strolled to see the rest of the place. Outside the various rooms of different herbs and spices, the tour guide stopped them, and Benjamin braced himself to see how Skye would react when that door opened in a minute. Sure enough, up went the door, and Skye's eyes widened as the effect of a room packed with mint hit them full on.

It was almost enough to clear out sinuses if one breathed in too deeply. Skye took a deep breath and blinked. Benjamin chuckled.

"It's strong, right?"

"That's one word for it. Wow. I had no idea anything good could smell that much."

"Yeah. Getting to smell all the different ingredients is my other favorite part of coming out here. Maybe it's why I love experimenting with different spices when I cook. I can't resist seeing how something will taste when I find I like the smell of it."

"You cook?" Skye glanced over at him, astonishment on her face.

"Why is that so hard to believe?"

"I don't know. I just keep finding things out about you that I'm not expecting." She shrugged and moved into the next room to sniff that ingredient.

"Are you saying I'm not quite as dull and boring as you first thought?" He couldn't resist pressing her just a bit further.

Her lips pursed and then moved into a grin. "I plead the fifth. Isn't that what you lawyers say?"

"I'm not that kind of an attorney, but I'll let you by with it for now."

"Not that kind—" Her question was cut short as they wandered into the room where the boxes were assembled, and the noise of that plus the tour guide was too much to hold a conversation.

Soon after that, the tour was over, and they exited to the gift shop. Skye meandered through, touching mugs, sniffing boxes of tea—something she probably wouldn't have done before this—and admiring a small stuffed version of the Sleepytime bear.

He pointed to a sign that marked a bin of tea fifty percent off. "Want to take some with you?"

"No letting me ease into this, huh?" One corner of her mouth lifted.

"I just noticed that the blueberry one was included in the sale."

"It was okay, Benjamin, but I probably won't go making myself a cup this evening." She pressed her hand on his bicep and then moved on to look at something else.

The spot on his arm remained warm despite her no longer touching it. And even though he hadn't completely won her over, she hadn't said she'd never again try tea, so it was close enough to a win to count. He picked up a few flavors he knew his mom would like and added the bear Skye had admired as an impulse buy.

Bag of goodies in hand, he walked her back out to the lobby. "There's a big Sleepytime bear in that chair. I could take your picture with it, if you want. You could even put your hair net back on."

"Ugh. No hair nets. Though I'm sure my hair is a disaster now." She poked at the bun, but the disheveled look of it was rather charming.

She did go over and sit by the bear, but then she shook her head and pulled him down on the other side. "Ready?"

Though her arms were shorter than his, she seemed to have the perfect angle for selfies, and she quickly snapped a few of them with the bear between them. He'd never been one for taking pictures of himself, but if she would always be in the photo, too, he could find himself getting used to it. And the multiple meanings behind that thought had him reeling a bit.

Because she'd declared she never wanted a real relationship or anything it might lead to. So there was no point in going any further down this road they'd been traveling the last two weeks. She'd be here another month or so and then head on to her next adventure.

If only his heart agreed.

He dropped her back at Rain's house earlier than necessary. But although he cut their time together short today, something told him there'd be plenty of other opportunities to spend time together over the next month as his sister and cousin prepared to get married. And he couldn't work up the energy to feel one iota sorry about it.

6

Benjamin commanded his eyes to quit searching the church building for a head full of long, blonde hair, but his gaze continued to disobey. It didn't help that Amelia's list of wedding gifts received over the weekend wasn't holding his attention much. Why did anyone need a slow cooker *and* an instant cooker?

There.

Skye wore a bright blue sundress with some sort of fluttery details at the shoulders that gave sneaky peeks of the skin underneath. Her hair was braided and draped to hang down her front. She followed Rain and Jeremiah in without glancing left or right. Was he the only one who continued to look for excuses to see the other?

"Oh, is that Rain's sister?" Amelia's question cut into his staring.

"It is. Skye."

"Skye, huh?" Something in Amelia's voice drew his attention back to her and her classic smirk.

"Yes. Why did you say it like that?"

"Why couldn't you take your eyes off of her?" Amelia crossed her arms over her chest. "And why did you say her name as if it were almost sacred?"

"Oh, please. You're imagining things."

"Mm. We'll see about that." Amelia tugged her purse up higher on her shoulder and sauntered in the direction of Skye. "I need to ask Rain something anyway. Come introduce me."

Of all the things he wished, introducing his sister to Skye wasn't anywhere on the list. Yet, here he was. Probably only prove Amelia's point if he refused. He swallowed a sigh and dodged a few elderly ladies to catch up with his sister.

"Rain." Amelia's voice was that of the perky bride—something Benjamin hoped would tone down after the wedding. Not that he wasn't glad she was happy, but it got a bit old.

"Hi, Amelia. Did you have a nice shower yesterday?" Rain clasped his sister's hands with a squeeze. "Sorry I couldn't come. I was working another wedding."

"It was great. This church has such a giving heart. Clark and I feel spoiled and loved right now, for sure."

Rain beamed a smile right back at Amelia. "I'm so glad. I left my gift out on the foyer table. I wasn't sure if I'd see you this morning or not."

"I just happened to see you guys walk in." Amelia widened her eyes at Benjamin and then glanced at Skye before blinking at him once more.

Was he supposed to know what that meant?

"Have you met my sister, yet?" Rain drew the attention back her way.

Oh. Right. Amelia had wanted Benjamin to introduce her to Skye. Oops.

"Hi." Amelia thrust her hand toward Skye. "I'm Amelia. Benjamin's sister."

"The bride, right?" Skye gave one of those grins that said

she found something funny but wasn't about to let anyone else in on the joke. "I've heard a few things about your wedding. He keeps using you as an excuse to come by Happily Ever After."

"He does, huh?" Amelia sent another I-think-I-know-more-than-I-really-do looks his way.

"I believe you were the one who begged me to go the other day and return that huge flower notebook. And you had me go get it in the first place." He raised an eyebrow. "I didn't ask for it."

"Maybe he didn't ask for the excuse to come by, but he did take advantage of it to ask Skye to go hang out yesterday morning." Rain's stage whisper might as well have been a shout. So much for her being on his side in this craziness.

"Oh, really?" Amelia smiled as if someone just bought the ridiculously priced robot vacuum on her wedding registry. "Hanging out? Like a date?"

"I'm just being a friendly tour guide. Skye's never seen Boulder before, so we went to Pearl Street for dinner the other night. And by Mork and Mindy's house."

"You did not!" Amelia rolled her eyes. "You're such a nerd."

"It's a landmark!"

Amelia shook her head and exchanged a glance with Rain. "Did she even know anything about the old show?"

"Well, no, but that doesn't make it less impressive."

Amelia placed a hand on Skye's arm. "I'm so sorry. If you need someone else to show you around, let me know. I can do better than Mork and Mindy's house."

"I didn't mind. It was practically on our way back to Rain's, anyway." Skye shrugged. "And he took me by Celestial Seasonings yesterday. That was sort of neat."

"No hikes? I mean, we're sort of known for our mountains."

"We've only been out twi—"

"I'm really not a hi—"

He and Skye started at the same time and cut off when they realized the other was speaking.

He motioned to her. "You first."

"I'm not really a hiker. More of a beach and shopping kind of girl. But the mountains are pretty." Skye's gaze moved to the front of the auditorium for a moment. "Oh, looks like they're about to start."

A quick glance confirmed it.

"Since Mom's working the nursery today, why don't we just slide in next to them?" Amelia pointed to the end of the pew on the other side of Skye. "Clark is running late, but there's enough room for him to fit when he gets here."

Awkward, thy name is a meddling sister who thinks just because she's found her happily ever after, everyone else should.

But there wasn't much else to do. No other seats were available nearby, and the song leader was about to start. Benjamin scooted in and left about a foot between himself and Skye. Then, Amelia sat beside him and nudged him back a few inches. He sent a probably awkward smile Skye's way and then focused on the front. Hopefully the worship service would be interesting and moving enough to keep his attention off the pretty girl beside him.

Skye's voice was a rich alto, and it blended well with her sister's higher notes. Benjamin found the beauty of their singing added something to the worship and settled in to enjoy. Clark slid in during the second song, pushing Amelia nearer, which forced Benjamin to close the gap between himself and Skye even more.

He hadn't had any problems with being close to her the day before when they toured the factory. Why was it awkward and uncomfortable now? Because of his matchmaking sister?

"Good morning, everyone." Bill, their preacher, got up, a

big smile on his face. "I'm so glad you're all here today. We're continuing our study of the letters to the Thessalonians. Today, we'll be in second Thessalonians chapter three."

Benjamin flipped his Bible open to the scripture while Skye scrolled through her phone app. He got there first. His finger traced down past the verses the sermon had been on the week before and then froze when the heading caught his attention. "Warning Against Idleness."

Sure enough, as Bill read through the passage, Benjamin wondered how these verses would be taken by the one sitting next to him. Where would Bill go with this lesson? And would it help or hurt Skye's aversion to finding a job?

Skye kept herself from scooting closer to Rain as Benjamin's arm brushed against hers once again. His cologne was something spicy, and she hadn't noticed it before today. Probably because she hadn't let herself get too close to him for long. How had they ended up crammed into this pew?

"Let's dig into some of these verses deeper." The preacher waved his open Bible around, as if to scatter the Word throughout the auditorium. "Obviously, the Thessalonian church had been having some issues with idleness. Of course, they weren't the only ones.

"Over in first Timothy, Paul admonishes the younger widows to not be included in the ones taken care of by the church, because he says it allowed them to learn to be idle, which could lead to them being gossips and busybodies. Whew! Talk about a quick slope downhill!"

Skye kept herself from rolling her eyes, but just barely. This didn't apply to her because she wasn't a widow. Or a busybody.

"But the Thessalonian church seemed to have a worse case than others. Because they were already admonished once in their first letter to not be idle. And now, here they are again. This time getting a whole paragraph—at least in my Bible—devoted to it."

The preacher held his Bible up as if people could read it from where they sat. He tapped the page. "'Now we command you, brothers, in the name of our Lord Jesus Christ, that you keep away from any brother who is walking in idleness and not in accord with the tradition that you received from us.' And how did Paul and his friends act when they were there? He says they weren't idle. They 'worked day and night' and didn't even let them give them bread without paying for it. Why do you think it mattered?"

Why did it matter? Skye resisted the urge to flip over to something else on her phone. That was the biggest problem with using an app instead of a real Bible.

Benjamin shifted again, this time bumping his knee into hers. He cast her an apologetic look and then focused on his own scriptures. Had this sermon only been going for ten minutes?

"Well, Paul tells us right here. They did it 'not because we do not have that right, but to give you in ourselves an example to imitate. For even when we were with you, we would give you this command: If anyone is not willing to work, let him not eat. For we hear that some among you walk in idleness, not busy at work, but busybodies.'"

The preacher shook his head and tutted. "There's that word again. Looks like not working tends to lead to sin, what do you think?"

Not working leads to sin? He was really making that leap of logic? Skye agreed that people with too much time on their hands could get into trouble, but that wasn't just because they weren't working. It was because they weren't doing *anything*. She didn't fall into that category.

"I mean, he said it right there. 'If anyone is not willing to work, let him not eat.' Sounds like he really wants the people to work. He ends that section with 'Now such persons we command and encourage in the Lord Jesus Christ to do their work quietly and to earn their own living.' Then, he goes on to remind them to have nothing to do with people who don't follow that advice—to warn them as brothers."

Not eating was beyond serious. Skye couldn't go more than four or five hours without eating most days. But this wasn't about her—even if she didn't have a full-time job yet. She was working.

"Why wouldn't people want to work?" The preacher set his Bible down and paced the stage. "There's probably any of number of reasons, just like today. Some people back then actually thought they were just supposed to wait for Jesus to come back, so why bother taking a job? Others took advantage of the church taking care of them, like those widows over in first Timothy."

Benjamin had to be the squirmiest guy Skye had ever sat beside during a church service. Or was it her who had bumped him this time? Either way, there didn't seem to be enough room between the pews for all these legs.

"We have similar situations today. People who live off the government or churches or friends or family because they don't want to have to earn their own living. And I'm not talking about those who are physically unable. I'm talking about people who are capable, but lazy. But there's another verse about that.

"Proverbs twelve verse twenty-four says, 'The hand of the diligent will rule, while the slothful will be put to forced labor.' What does that mean?"

Skye tried to chase the image of sloths ruling the world out of her head. They were really cute, but they didn't move very fast. Was that really what he'd said?

"It means they who work for it are going to be the leaders. And those who are lazy or slothful—well, they might end up doing things they don't want to. Like forced labor."

Forced labor was something Skye could empathize with. Wasn't that exactly what her father was pushing her into right now? As if nothing in the world mattered more than making money—including how she did it.

Rain nudged her and Skye straightened up. Had she been doing something wrong, or was Rain trying to call her attention to the sermon? Either way, it wasn't appreciated. She scowled at her older sister. Rain simply lifted a brow and returned her focus to the last few words of the message.

Somehow, Skye kept from cheering as they all stood to sing the final hymn. She'd made it through the lesson, though from Rain's expression, a follow-up might happen during lunch. It was almost enough to tempt her to see if Benjamin wanted to go somewhere instead. But not quite.

No. When he'd walked over with his plaid bowtie this morning, it had taken all her willpower to keep from laughing. Strange that she'd spent so much time with him over the last few weeks, considering he was not her type at all. The complete opposite, if truth were told.

"Amen." Benjamin's low murmur next to her brought her back to reality.

Oops. She'd completely zoned out during the closing prayer. Too late now. She'd talk to God more later. He'd understand.

"Rain." Amelia leaned over the pew and called past her brother and Skye. "Can you talk for a minute, or do I need to come by the shop this week? We might be changing our minds about writing our own vows."

Skye hid her discomfort at Amelia's desire to basically make Rain work on a Sunday—her one day off each week. Shouldn't work have boundaries so the rest of life was free to simply be enjoyed? Or did Skye want too much? It didn't seem to faze Rain.

"You got lunch plans?" Benjamin followed her out into the aisle so Amelia and Rain could talk.

"Rain said something about Italian." Skye hefted her handbag onto her shoulder but didn't offer anything else. Even though she'd contemplated asking him to go somewhere, the reality was, she wasn't sure what she wanted. And there was something too serious here. Maybe Rain was right the other day, and she should just back off.

"Bennie, I just had a great idea." Amelia touched both their arms and grinned as if she'd been named queen for the day.

Bennie? Skye mouthed the nickname but couldn't accept it. It didn't fit him.

His lips twitched as if he knew what she was thinking. "What's that, sis?"

"You don't have your plus one yet for my wedding, right? And we're only a month away. Why not ask Skye?"

Did crickets usually take over church buildings? There was definitely room for their song as everyone in their group went completely silent. Only Amelia still smiled.

Benjamin cleared his throat and straightened his already straight bowtie. "I'm thinking Rain probably needs Skye's help that day, Amelia. I mean, that's sort of why Skye is here this summer. To work with Rain."

"Oh, right!" Amelia blinked. "I didn't even think about that."

"Besides, she'll probably be weddinged out by then. Won't

want to attend one as a near-stranger's date." Benjamin tossed her a smile she couldn't quite interpret.

Skye had been trying to formulate a way to bow out easily, but now that the chance was denied her, she couldn't chase away a bit of disappointment. Surely she didn't really want to go to a wedding as Benjamin's date. Wasn't that something only real couples did? And he was only one of her FLIRTS.

"Most of the work is done by the actual wedding. I do a few things like tell bridesmaids when to walk or make sure the photographer is in place, but I should be okay to do all that by myself, if Skye needs to be off." Rain shrugged.

Skye couldn't tell if her sister was trying to smooth things over with Amelia or if she was changing her stance from before. Life wasn't supposed to be this confusing.

And now, everyone stared at her. Had she missed an actual question? Because she couldn't remember Benjamin actually asking out loud if she'd be his date to his sister's wedding. She shifted and tossed a grin she hoped came off as carefree.

"I mean, we'll see if he still needs a date by then. He might find someone else to ask in the next month. I don't want to tie him down."

Was that collective sigh out loud or in her head? Either way, this day had been way too awkward all around. When Jeremiah motioned for them to head out for lunch, she was nothing but relieved.

At least, that's what she told herself. Though she could swear Benjamin watched her all the way through the door. As if he'd wanted to take her to lunch—and maybe the wedding —but didn't feel he should. Was that what she wanted too?

If not, why did she miss him as she ate her pasta?

7

"Whatcha workin' on?" Rain turned to Skye after she'd escorted a bride to the door.

"Sorry. I finished up the invoices, and you were still with the future Mrs. Bowers, so I thought I'd skim this job site for a few minutes."

"Not a worry." Rain came up beside her and leaned in to see the screen. "Actually, I'm rather glad to see you taking some initiative. Is this because of the sermon on Sunday?"

So Rain *had* been hinting at her needing to do this when she nudged her two mornings ago. Skye let the frustration roll off her shoulders. Rain was still in mothering mode, and nothing would change that.

"Actually, it's because I only have six weeks left, if you're sticking to our original plan." Skye tapped the calendar on the desk beside her. "And so, I decided to at least see what's out there."

"And?"

"Nothing that sounds like anything I want to do." She slumped and rested her chin on her fists.

65

"What parameters did you give a potential job? Are you only looking around St. Louis or other places too?" Rain took over the mouse and scrolled up to see what all Skye had entered.

"Believe it or not, I know how to do a job search." Skye wrestled the mouse back. "And I haven't tried much yet. I only started five minutes ago."

"I bet there's something out there, then." Rain tapped her shoulder before turning to walk up the stairs. "Just keep trying different things until that perfect position pops up."

Perfect position. As if there were such a thing. Skye scoffed at all the office manager and administrative assistant listings on the site. Boring. Life behind a desk with a phone to her ear all day sounded less than exciting.

Why had she agreed to take all those college business classes their father recommended? How handy were they really if she didn't want any of the jobs they qualified her for? Not that she had a clue what kind of occupation she wanted.

Wasn't that one of the reasons to go to college in the first place? To figure out what to do with the rest of her life? Instead, she sat here hating everything about her future, or lack thereof.

It was enough to make a girl wish a certain groomsman would walk in with some random excuse for swinging by, only to take the opportunity to suggest something fun. Or if only there were a place that would pay her to have fun. That would be even better. Way less complicated than relying on some up-and-coming attorney who had a bicycle as a steed and a '57 Chevy truck as his backup.

"You could always start your own event planning busi-ness." Rain came down with a box of what looked to be tulle. "Just not around here, please. I don't want the competition."

"Afraid I might be able to gain more business than you? Please." Skye scoffed. "I don't even like weddings."

"You keep saying that. But I could've sworn there were some sparks flying between you and a certain attorney on Sunday." Rain set the box down. "The one you swore knew you didn't like anything that smelled or looked like a relationship."

"I've told him." Skye's phone dinged and she cringed at the name on the screen.

> Status report on your job plan?

Her father's words didn't even read like he was related to her—more like a boss. Or dictator.

> I'm working on it.

Hopefully that reply would satisfy him for today.
No such luck.

> Have you sent off a single application? Put your resume out there for any companies to find?

If she didn't bother to respond, would he let her get away with it?

"Who's texting you? Not the attorney, right?" Rain laughed.

"No. Much worse." She flipped her phone face down and readjusted her search parameters.

"Worse? As if getting a text from Benjamin Smith would be a bad thing. He might take you out to dinner again and save you from my lack of desire to cook." Rain nipped Skye's phone before she could stop her. "Dad? Dad's texting you?"

"Our father seems to think I need supervising. Or that I

don't take his threats seriously enough or something. As if I'd let him take Rosie away. I'll find something before my time is up." Skye gave the mouse a few extra-hard clicks as she scrolled down a list even worse than the previous one.

"You know he only wants to make sure you'll be okay. He's doing this out of love."

"Love." Skye practically spit the word out. "Please. He's doing this because he doesn't want to have any responsibility for me anymore. I'm nothing but a liability. A monthly expense he's tired of paying."

"Autumn Skye Jones!" Rain pulled out her best mom voice and propped her fists on her hips. "You did not just say that about our dad."

"I did too." She gave up and closed out the job search website. "And you know it's true."

"He loves you, Skye. He wants what's best for you, which is for you to go ahead and grow up. Learn to take care of yourself. I thought bringing you out here for the summer might help, but now I'm not so sure. Instead, I think it just bought you two more months of not facing reality."

Jerking her purse off the floor, Skye jumped to her feet and rummaged for her keys. "I guess everything I've done for you the last few weeks hasn't been real work? That me sitting here searching for jobs I don't actually want isn't real enough? What else do I have to do?"

"Skye, stop."

"Nope. If you don't have anything else for me to do today, I'm heading out early. Just take it out of my paycheck, if you need to." She jerked her phone from Rain's hand and stormed out the door, barely missing taking out a teenage guy walking down the sidewalk.

The thin mountain air did nothing to help her fill her lungs as she threw herself into Rosie and gunned the engine. Rain was supposed to be on her side. Or at least commiserate. Instead, she agreed with their father? In his strict, demeaning, bossy ways? Well, maybe she'd find something else to earn a few dollars for the remainder of the summer.

She didn't have to stay and take this, that was for sure.

Though she didn't know where she was going, either.

Benjamin straightened the papers on the will he'd just prepared for the Davidson family. They were expecting their first child in a few months and wanted to make sure a guardian was named, just in case. Helping bring some peace into the world of couples young and old, in all walks of life, was his favorite part of this job.

Soon, he should probably talk to Amelia about doing a will too. Nothing fancy. But a basic will would cover any problems that might arise and make sure a safety net was in place.

He shook his head. Young couples about to be married didn't want to think about needing powers of attorney or last wills and testaments. No. If Amelia were to be believed, she and Clark would live forever in their state of bliss.

Could he stand her that long?

Maybe he'd find his own happily ever after before too much longer and join his sister in the state of euphoria she seemed to stay in all the time now. A certain blonde flitted through his head, but he shook that thought loose. No. Skye had made it abundantly clear she was off limits in the marriage department.

"Only FLIRTS for her." He wrinkled his nose as he muttered the words under his breath.

His sister might think Benjamin and Skye would make a good couple, but he knew better than his meddling sibling. It's like she thought he was incapable of finding his own forever love. Not that he hadn't considered it before now—he was the older sibling, after all. But he simply hadn't met anyone he wanted to spend the rest of his life with up to now.

"Have a good evening, Smith." Marston, one of the senior attorneys, rapped his knuckles on Benjamin's door as he walked by.

He was leaving early. Or not. Benjamin's eyes widened at the numbers on the clock. That's what happened when his last appointment of the day didn't start until four.

He straightened his desk and gathered a few things he needed to take with him. Nothing much, because most of the time, his work stayed at the office. But he wanted to work on some wording for a complicated trust he needed in a few days. With all that family's branches, their money would be distributed a million ways, and one wrong phrase might mess it all up and send it to probate court for months.

As he pushed through the door, his phone rang. Rain. He frowned. Hadn't they already finalized his parts for the weddings?

"Hello."

"Benjamin. Oh, good!" Rain's voice sounded a bit frantic.

"What's up? Something wrong with my bridezilla of a sister?" He chuckled as he unlocked his bike from beside the office building.

"No. Unfortunately, I was calling to see if you'd heard anything from *my* sister this afternoon."

"Skye? No. Why?"

Rain released a breath so long he wondered if she had any left. "We had a big fight about an hour ago. I couldn't get away from the shop right then because I had an appointment, and by the time I left, I thought maybe she'd be back at the house, but there's no sign of her. Jeremiah has baseball until around seven this evening, and I couldn't think of anyone else to call."

Benjamin looped his messenger bag over his head to hang across his chest. "Any idea where she might have gone? Maybe to get dinner?"

"I guess that's a possibility, but I seriously don't know all the places she's been around here. The only times she's really gone out anywhere were with you."

Memories flitted through his head of the few occasions he'd had to spend any time with her. "I can check Pearl Street. We ate dinner down there one night."

"Would you? I was trying to look her up on my app, but I think maybe she's turned her phone off or something, because it's not pulling her up."

"I'll head that way now." He slipped his helmet on and clicked the straps in place. "Hang in there, Rain. It'll be okay."

As he maneuvered through traffic, he kept an eye out for the little red convertible. Curiosity about why they had fought warred with wondering where she might head to cool off. Assuming she wished to cool off and not simply fan the flames.

He parked his bike at the first rack on Pearl Street and mingled with the foot traffic, heavier during the dinner hour despite it being a weeknight. Couples and families all loved to come down here because of the numerous restaurants and safety in no cars driving through. A lot of the benches were occupied, but not by anyone with long blonde hair.

Wait. Maybe.

He worked his way over to a bench near a fountain. The girl sitting there wore a long blue skirt with a ruffle at the bottom, a blouse with lacy accents, and had her blonde hair wrapped in a braid around her head, like a crown. Her gaze was fixed on the mountains in the distance, and she didn't move until he slid onto the wooden seat beside her.

"Oh!" She startled, an expression of recognition flashed over her features, and then she moved as if to leave.

He grabbed her wrist and tugged, strong enough to encourage her to sit back down, but not to hurt her. "Please don't go."

For another second or two, she resisted before slumping back down. "How'd you find me?"

"Your sister mentioned you hadn't been any place except with me, so I figured this was probably where you'd escape, since you don't like tea." He slowly released his hold on her arm, half afraid she might bolt if he let go completely.

"So, Rain did put you up to it?"

"She called because she was worried and didn't know who else could help." He typed out a quick message to Rain to let her know he'd found Skye, but not where.

"Did you just tell her where I was?"

"No. Just that you were safe." He tucked his phone back in his pocket. "Have you eaten?"

"Just some ice cream." She still wouldn't meet his eyes.

"Well, that won't do at all." He stood and offered a hand. "Come on."

She frowned at his fingers. "Where are we going?"

"To get dinner, of course. Do you want Indian again or something different?"

With a shrug, she rose, her arms crossed over her chest. "I don't care. Honestly, nothing sounds good."

"I know just the place." He drew one of her arms loose and through his, then headed them a few blocks farther down, a bit worried that none of her playfulness and flirty nature shone through.

Into the café and over to a table near the window, he continued to hold onto her, lest she pull loose and head off again. "Voila."

She picked up a menu and then set it down without even glancing it over. "This is ridiculous. I don't even want anything."

"Their pot pie is good. And their fried chicken." He tapped the list in front of her. "Or mac and cheese. You need some soul food."

"I didn't think you were allowed to have soul food in Boulder. Doesn't it have too many carbs and artificial flavors?" There was a bit of her spark back.

His lips twitched and he wiggled his eyebrows. "Try it and see."

This time she actually looked at the menu, and when the waitress came to take their order, he was pleased to hear her ask for the macaroni along with a piece of chicken. He wouldn't tell her that they made it as healthy as possible. The food would speak for itself.

"Now that you've found me—and forced me to a place with more than ice cream—I suppose your job is to return me to my rightful owner?" Skye played with the bundle of silverware.

"Rightful owner?" He tilted his head. "I didn't realize you were being treated like property."

Skye's lips pursed and then relaxed again. "If I were, you could take my *owners* to court and sue them for me, right?"

"Afraid not." He leaned back in his chair. "I don't practice that kind of law."

"Don't practice—" Skye finally gave him her full attention. "What do you mean? I thought all lawyers could sue people."

"I guess I probably could, but I'd have to read up on it. It's not the area I'm licensed in. I focus more on estate planning and businesses."

"What does that mean?"

"Wills and trusts, powers of attorney, living wills, LLCs, S-

Corps, things like that." He waved his hand through the air. "A few of the attorneys at the firm deal with some family law, too, but it gets too messy for me."

"I thought you said you became a lawyer because you liked to argue." She crossed her arms again and raised an eyebrow.

"That's what led me to law in the first place. But then, once I got into it and discovered the various types of law, I decided I'd much rather deal with issues that don't require an argument every day. Arguing is fun in certain circumstances, but it can also get really old, really fast." He leaned forward and spread his hands on the table. "What I do helps people have peace of mind or fewer tax repercussions. And that's rewarding."

"Your job sounds even more boring now than it did when I first heard about it."

"Your opinion." He leaned back as the waitress brought their plates of steaming food. "Doesn't mean I have to agree."

"There's that arguing you like to do so much, huh?"

He shrugged and then held out his hands. "Let's pray, and then we can dig in."

She hesitated only a moment before sliding her fingers into his.

"Father God, we thank you for this beautiful summer day. Thank you for friends to spend time with. Thank you for this food. Please be with Skye and her family and help them find peace as they work through whatever is going on tonight. Bless us all as we try to be a light for You. Thank you, Lord. In Jesus' name, Amen."

Skye lifted her head slowly. "You're not even going to ask what Rain and I fought over?"

"It's your story to tell if you want to. Mostly, I'm concerned that you were all alone and hurting. I'm here to be a friend.

Take that for whatever you will." He motioned to her macaroni. "Eat."

The words came easily out of his mouth, but inside was turmoil. She was hurting but didn't seem to want to admit it even to herself. How could he help her if she wouldn't let him in?

And if she did let him in, would he be able to get back out unscathed?

8

"Do you need a place to stay tonight?" Benjamin held the door for Skye as they left the café.

She stared off in the direction of Rain's house. "I don't know."

"She won't kick you out just because you had an argument." Benjamin didn't want to press too hard but also wanted to make sure she saw things with open eyes. "She loves you and wants what's best for you. But you can stay at my place if you need a little more time before you face her again."

"Your place?" Skye frowned. "I thought you lived with your family."

"I have a townhouse not too far from here. All mine. But some weekends I go stay at my parents' just to be around them." He stuck his hands in his pockets. "I can stay at Mom's tonight if you want to borrow my place."

So much for not adding to her turmoil. Her face wasn't hiding anything today like it had the first few times they met. Instead, it was an open book of uncertainty and pain. What caused her to hurt like that?

"I shouldn't kick you out of your own house." She tugged on a strand of hair that had come loose from her braid. "Besides, all my clothes are back at Rain's."

"True. While I bet you'd look great in one of my suits, you'd probably insist they're not your style." Had he seriously just said that? And now he couldn't chase that image from his mind. Ugh.

"No." Skye's eyes held mischief as she reached up and tapped his shoulder. "Besides, they'd probably be too big."

A lump of tension filled his throat and then eased down into the middle of his stomach. Had the temperature just gone up about eighty degrees? He tugged at his collar, but the top two buttons were already undone.

"Thanks for dinner, Benjamin." Skye released a big sigh. "I'm sure I wasn't on the agenda for your evening."

She might not have started there, but he couldn't imagine spending it any other way. More and more, his evenings looked empty without a certain blonde's company. Not that he could tell her he'd like to add her to his agenda more often than not.

"Need a lift?"

"I parked back down at that end somewhere." She pointed in the direction of his bike.

"I'll walk you back, at least."

"It's a free country."

His lips twitched, but he controlled his chuckle before it escaped. The armor was slipping back into place. She would be fine. Was it because of the time spent with him? Or just because she'd finally cooled off from earlier?

They walked quietly for a few minutes, and then an idea popped in his head. Would she go for it? It seemed like something right up her alley.

He cleared his throat. "Speaking of agendas ..."

"Uh, oh. Agenda sounds rather stuffy and boring."

"Okay, *calendar* or *schedule* if you prefer. *Plans*? A date by any other name is just as sweet, to completely misquote the bard."

"A date?" She froze and stared at him with big, blue-grey eyes.

"Not a date-date." He swished his hand through the air as if he could sweep away the complete mess he was making of this.

Crossing her arms, she raised an eyebrow and waited.

Here went nothing. "There's a group at church—people our age—getting together Thursday evening. They're calling it a thrift store date night. We start at the thrift store and everyone gets a different person to shop for. We have to find the ... most interesting outfit we can for that person. Then we swing by the church building to change into said clothes before going out to a fun restaurant for dinner. Afterward we have a short devotional in the church courtyard."

Her stance hadn't changed as he described the event. Had he been wrong? Was it too much like a real date? Or was she still considering leaving after that fight with Rain?

He squeezed the back of his neck and grimaced. "No big deal. I know things are sort of up in the air with you right now."

"Do we get to pick who we shop for?" A smile that could only be described as wicked spread across her mouth.

He pinched his lips together for a few seconds to keep from beaming. "Maybe."

"When and where do we meet?"

"I can pick you up if you want." Too forward! "Then you won't have to worry about finding places you've never been, I mean."

"Are you insinuating I'm the kind of girl who gets lost easily?" She propped her fists on her hips.

"Are you putting words in my mouth?" He shot back.

"Truce?" Her hand shot out like a peace offering.

"Truce." He wrapped his fingers around hers and gave a firm pump.

"I'm not a dumb blonde, you know." She started meandering toward her car again.

"I never said you were."

"And yet, you act like I need to be taken care of. Like I'm incapable of doing anything myself."

Her lack of permanent employment ran through his head, but he locked his tongue over the thought and shoved it aside. Now was not the time to point something like that out. Instead, he needed to continue to make peace.

"Terribly sorry you feel I'm coddling you." He tugged her arm before she walked into another couple coming from the other direction. "I don't mean it to come across that way."

She snickered. "Who am I kidding? I can't even walk straight."

"In your defense, they weren't watching where they went either."

"Thanks."

Before he was ready, they reached the end of the shopping area. Her bright red car was easily visible a few feet away. He unlocked his bike and walked it over to where she was parked.

"You sure you're good tonight?"

"I'll be fine. If nothing else, at least I can escape to the basement, and she won't bother me." Skye leaned against her car door. "Rain tries too much to be a mother to me. And I'd much rather have a sister. I feel like she'd be more understanding and on my side that way."

"I guess I can see that." He fiddled with his helmet strap. "But maybe you need to step back and look at things from her angle. Maybe she doesn't even realize how she comes across."

Skye pouted her lips out in the most distracting way. "Maybe."

"If you need anything at all, let me know." He opened her car door for her and helped her in. "Otherwise, I'll see you Thursday evening, if not before at Wednesday Bible study."

"What time?"

"A little after five?" He motioned to his watch. "I'm hoping to slip out of the office a bit early that afternoon."

"See you then." She shot him a saucy smile. "I can't wait to find something amazing for you to wear. I'm an excellent shopper."

"Just be careful." His finger tapped her nose. "You have to wear whatever I pick out for you too."

"I've seen how you dress. I'll be okay unless I die from boredom."

"Challenge accepted." He backed away. "Go ahead and get out of here so I can safely ride my bike home."

"Ha!" She threw the laugh over her shoulder as she pulled out into traffic.

Her feistiness was back. That had to be a good sign. But he shot a text off to Rain anyway, to give her a head's up that the storm was headed her way. Because Skye was as tempestuous as the afternoon downpours that came over the mountains on a hot day. No telling how she would blow.

It was something he never knew he liked until now.

Skye froze as Rain rose from her spot on the sofa the moment she walked in the door.

"You're back."

"Is that okay?" Skye held her breath, unsure what kind of mood her sister was in. Benjamin had said Rain was worried about her, but nothing indicated it now. If anything, her posture radiated an angry aura.

"Of course, it's okay." Rain's hands flopped at her sides. "This is your home for the summer."

"I wasn't sure the offer still stood after earlier."

Rain quite literally deflated as she collapsed on the couch. "I wasn't sure you still wanted to be here."

Skye nudged her over a few inches and then snuggled in beside her, head on Rain's shoulder. "I said several things I shouldn't have. For instance, I really do still need to work for you until I can figure out something else."

Her sister's huff sounded enough like a laugh that Skye considered it safe to keep going.

"And all my clothes are here. Not to mention it's in my price range."

"You're living here for free."

"Exactly." Skye poked Rain in the side.

Rain snagged a pillow and bopped Skye on the head. "Just don't run out like that again. I get that we don't see eye to eye on things, though I can't figure out why you think Dad's out to get you."

"Because he is." The words were under Skye's breath, but as close as they were sitting, Rain could hear.

"He's not, but we're not going to argue about it anymore tonight." Rain held up a finger when Skye opened her mouth. "Off limits for at least twenty-four hours until we both cool off some more."

Skye nodded.

"Now, let me assure you that you still have a job. I know I'm good at what I do, but there is absolutely no way I can pull off four weddings in the next three weeks without help."

"I'm at your service. Except for Thursday night, evidently."

"Thursday night?" Rain raised an eyebrow.

"Benjamin said a bunch of people from church are getting together to do one of those thrift-store dates and then eat dinner and have a devotional. He invited me to join them."

Rain leaned back and stared at Skye.

"What?" Skye rubbed at her face, wondering if she'd smeared cheese sauce or something.

"Benjamin, the guy you're not interested in dating, Benjamin?"

"Ugh. It's a church function. Not really a date. We're literally going to wear the ugliest outfits imaginable."

"And, of course, you can't date anyone in a group setting or ugly clothes." Her sister rolled her eyes and meandered into the kitchen. "Have you reminded him of your stance on relationships?"

"I didn't think I needed to." Skye followed and grabbed a glass for water. "Besides, you're the one who sent him to find me this afternoon. I didn't ask for that. I would've come back eventually."

Though probably a lot hungrier because she wouldn't have eaten anything but the ice cream. Beside the point. As was the way he made her laugh and smile when she didn't want to.

"I wouldn't have sent him if you hadn't run off without a word of where you were going. And you turned off your cell phone so I couldn't even check the app." Rain pulled a pint of chocolate caramel ice cream out of the freezer and grabbed a spoon.

"I didn't want to get texts from you or our father, so, yes, I turned off my phone for a while. I'm not exactly a teenager anymore. I was okay. Just down on Pearl Street."

"But I didn't know that." Rain took a big bite of the dessert and savored it for a second. "And Benjamin was the only other one who had spent time with you here. I figured he'd have a better guess about the places you knew besides my house and the shop.”

“Well, he found me. He made sure I had a real dinner. And here I am, back again. No need to worry.”

“Lots of needs to worry, actually.” Waving her spoon around, Rain gave Skye a look that had all kinds of warnings attached. “Benjamin is a really great guy, and I don’t want to see him get hurt just because he’s falling into your web.”

“Web? Now I’m a spider?” Skye squawked. “I don’t weave webs. I was completely up front with him. I don’t do anything more serious than my FLIRTS. And he still invited me. That means he knows the rules.”

Rain shook her head. “Just please be careful. For both your sakes.”

Oh, how she wanted to protest again. To say she was always careful. That she never let it go further than fun. But a tiny niggle in her chest wouldn’t let the words come out.

What was going on?

“It’s just a church function.” She said the words aloud for her own benefit as much as her sister’s. “What could possibly happen?”

“With you? Who knows?” Rain put the last little bit of ice cream back in the freezer.

“Thanks for your trust.” Skye poked at the braid that had started hurting hours before. “I’m going to grab a shower and then catch up on social media and stuff. I’ll see you in the morning.”

“I love you, you know.” Rain pressed a kiss to Skye’s head.

“I love you too.”

Head a bit clearer after her shower, Skye scrolled through the various posts of friends from that day. Not much new. Vacations. Kids. Engagements. Wait!

She moved the screen back up and chuckled. Bree and

Nathan were back together. Her plan had worked. Maybe she should be a matchmaker.

Nah. She'd never be able to put her heart into something she didn't want for herself. Not for people she didn't love like Bree.

"Still, it's a different kind of job. Wonder if there's something else out there just as fun."

"He'll be here." Rain covered Skye's fingers; she hadn't even realized she was tapping on the countertop.

"He said a little after five."

"And it's only five-fifteen now. There could be any number of reasons causing him to be a bit later than he meant to be."

Skye scowled. This was why she dreaded having a real job. It controlled your life. Made you miss out on the fun things. Because what else could have kept Benjamin from being here when he said he would?

The door opened, setting the bells to jingling. Benjamin strolled in, hands in his pockets, as if he were right on time. Did 'a little' mean something different to him than it did to her?

"Hey. You ready?"

Skye tapped a few more times, willing her jaw to relax. "Sure. Been ready."

He glanced at the clock on the wall behind her. "Yeah. Sorry. I left about five minutes later than I meant to, which means traffic was three times worse. Life in a city."

And his work being to blame was confirmed.

She shouldered her purse and climbed off the stool. "Let's go."

"Don't have too much fun, you two." Rain's warning followed them out onto the sidewalk.

"What was that supposed to mean?" Benjamin opened the passenger door of his truck for her.

"Who knows?" Except Skye knew. It was her sister's way of reminding her not to let things get any more serious between herself and Benjamin. As if she needed the warning.

"Since we're running a few minutes late, I let everyone know we'd meet them at the thrift store."

"Works for me. Ready to rock some amazing clothes?"

"Almost as ready to rock them as I am to see you in yours." He waggled his eyebrows before veering off to a part of town she hadn't explored yet.

Only a few minutes spent with Benjamin, and she was already relaxing and letting go of the earlier angst. Add in the thrill of bargain hunting and seeing him in something besides a button-up shirt and bowtie, and she practically bounced on her seat. Well, more than this truck normally sent her bumping, anyway.

"Here we are. Let the fun begin." Benjamin left his suitcoat in the truck and then offered his elbow to her.

Should she take it? Better than if he did that thing where he let his hand hover on the small of her back. She linked arms with him and tugged him toward the store.

"C'mon. Everyone else has a head start."

He laughed and pulled her to a stop between the men's and women's sections. "Now, don't forget. Fifteen-dollar maximum. And nothing immodest or with any improper slogans."

She rolled her eyes as she took in how the clothing was organized. Long-sleeved shirts, short-sleeved, button-down, sweaters, jackets, pants, and shorts. Various colors caught her eyes, and she grinned.

"Got it. Don't worry about me. I'm a great shopper."

"I think that might be what I'm worried about." He tugged her arm one more time as she started toward something particularly bright red on the other side of the closest rack. "Don't forget. You have to wear what I pick out."

"I'm a size small." She winked at him and then pulled free to explore.

A few familiar faces were around—the others in their group. She hadn't met many of them officially yet, but she recognized them from the few times she'd attended worship with Rain. And some of the items in their arms gave her hope to find something as amazing. One girl carried around a sleeve-less T-shirt that said "Heartbreaker" along with some very bright plaid shorts and what looked like suspenders.

Knowing Benjamin, he probably owned suspenders already. No. She needed something better. Hmm.

The T-shirts weren't giving her any thrills. And it was too hot for a sweater, though a few had a pattern straight out of the '80s. What else? She was sick of seeing him in dressy clothes and wanted something more laid-back.

Wow.

Was that a shirt with a cat face done in the style of Van Gogh's starry night? She picked it up with a giggle. But it was obviously too small. So much for that fabulous find.

Hmm. This might work.

Hawaiian-style shirt done in the most garrulous color combination she'd ever seen. Neon green, purple, and orange flowers filled the space, leaving no room for the eye to rest. But what to pair it with?

Ripped jeans? Maybe. Hunter green carpenter pants that zipped off? She could actually picture him in those. Or ... woah.

Old-school red swim trunks. Her lips spread in a grin far too wide for such a silly evening.

And she still had a bit of money left to spend. Time for some accessories.

High top sneakers, frayed around the edges, with a design done in sharpie. And they matched the size he'd given her. As she scanned the store one more time, just to make sure she hadn't missed anything better, her gaze caught on a rack of hats. Perfect.

Old-man golfing hat? Nah. Tractor green baseball cap with a fish on the front? She wouldn't pick that for her worst enemy. Hmm. Oh. That one. Perfect.

She twirled the pin-striped fedora around her finger and laughed out loud when she spotted the brown feather peeking out of the ribbon. Yes!

"What has you so happy?" Benjamin's voice right behind her startled her.

Her armload of clothing crashed around their feet.

"Sorry. I didn't realize you hadn't heard me come up." He lifted the shirt. "I'm feeling bright tonight, huh?"

"Isn't it great?" She couldn't control her smirk.

"It's something, all right."

She'd been so caught up in picking out everything for him to wear, she hadn't even thought to look and see what he was grabbing for her. He must've been faster than she was, because he held a plastic shopping bag over one arm as he picked up the sneakers between pinched fingers.

"Wow. I used to have a pair sort of like this in elementary school. Though not quite so ... unique." He turned them from side to side.

"I thought they rounded out the ensemble well." She accepted the things from him and carried them toward the checkout. "Ready to rock this outfit?"

"As ready as I'll ever be." He lifted a brow. "Though I'm not sure the world is quite ready to see that much of my pale legs."

She giggled and handed over her money. "Those shorts wouldn't let me pass them up."

He shook his head. "Hopefully the rest of our group won't be scandalized. I don't think I've had shorts that short since I was in kindergarten."

"Oh, please. Guys used to wear these all the time when my father was in school."

"Great. Now she's comparing me to her dad." He opened his truck door for her, and she couldn't stop laughing as he walked around.

"Do I get to see what you picked for me?" She wiggled her fingers his way as he slid into his side.

"Hmm. I think maybe we should prolong the anticipation." He stowed his bag behind his seat. "We're only a few minutes from the church building."

"Anticipation or dread?" No matter how she craned her neck, she couldn't see what the plastic hid. Maybe something pink? Or salmon?

"You sure you want to talk about dread? You don't have to wear those swim trunks."

Her giggles started all over again. "You're not ashamed of your legs, are you? Hiding chicken legs under all those fancy pants you wear?"

"Chicken legs!" He snorted. "I see what you think of me."

"What's the plan again? We change in the church building and then head out as a group for dinner?"

He nodded as he pulled into the parking lot. "And then we'll come back here and light up the firepit in the courtyard for s'mores. I think Keegan is doing a short devotional for us. And Samantha always takes pictures of these things. Because who doesn't want their embarrassing moment shared with the whole church on Sunday morning?"

"Do I get to see what I'm wearing now?" She hoped it fit. Maybe one of the other girls had safety pins, just in case.

"Okay. Here you are." He traded bags with her.

She held her breath as she moved the plastic aside and lifted out ... what was this thing? A suit? No. Just a paisley jacket ... with shoulder pads. Shoulder pads! And what else? A pleated skirt in a completely different shade of purple from the mauve and brown accents in the top part. Wow. A sunny-yellow camisole completed the main outfit, and a blue scarf and green shoes added an unnecessary pop of color.

"Perfect, right?" His smirk was well earned.

"I can't decide which of us is going to clash worse."

"Time to get dressed and see."

***

Benjamin liked to consider himself in pretty good shape. But these shorts ... man! He had to wiggle in ways no man should have to move to get the things all the way up. So much for eating much tonight.

"Whoa! I think I need some sunglasses. Cover those legs up, man!"

"I tried to tell her ..." Benjamin stepped out from the stall he'd been changing in.

"Not you." Alan pointed past him. "Keegan."

And suddenly Benjamin didn't feel so awkward anymore. Keegan was in some sort of tie-dye shirt with rips around the bottom. The frayed edges looked even stranger considering the way they hung over the top of a pair of what looked like cut off overalls. And they were cut several inches above his knees, leaving acres of pale white skin peeking out below.

"What was she thinking?" Keegan tugged on the denim.

"Yeah. I'm not feeling so bad about these pants." Alan spun in a circle, his legs clad in green corduroys.

"They look amazing with that plaid vest." Benjamin smirked.

"Don't get too cocky over there, surfer boy." Keegan motioned toward the outfit Benjamin wore. "You're setting a style I don't think many will copy."

"Oh, but this is the best part." He spun the fedora down his arm and then set it on his head at an angle. "I may keep this hat. I rather like it."

"It would look amazing with your normal bowties." Alan thumped Benjamin's chest.

"I'm glad someone likes my bowties."

"Trouble with your new girl?" Keegan opened the bathroom door.

"She's not my girl. Just a friend." Benjamin stepped out and scanned the others already gathered in the church foyer.

Was Skye out yet? All the crazy colors and patterns played tricks on his eyes and he looked back and forth at least three times before spotting the paisley coat.

Wow.

What he'd expected to look rather frumpy, Skye carried off with a flair. The scarf she'd used as a headband, and the skirt swirled around her calves, floating over those crazy green shoes. On anyone else, it would've appeared ridiculous. Skye made it seem natural.

She caught his eye and let out a whistle.

He swallowed and willed his heartrate back to a semi-normal pace. If she could play flirty and cool, he could too. Turning to the side, he struck a pose, showing off his biceps.

"Well, I'm impressed." She poked his arm and then shook her finger as if she'd hurt it. "You don't have chicken legs. Not even too pale. No one would think you slaved away in an office most of your life."

"Ha, ha." He popped the collar of his Hawaiian shirt. "An office job isn't nearly as bad as you think it is. I've been able to get away and hike several times already this summer."

She shook her head. "Hiking doesn't sound much more thrilling than sitting behind a desk to me."

"Maybe that's because you've never done it right."

"What? With the backpack thing and expensive boots and stuff?"

"No." He raised a brow. "With me."

A laugh burst from her lips. "Oh, man."

"What? You don't think I know how to have fun?"

"The verdict's still out."

"Ooh. Lawyer talk." He rubbed his hands together.

"Stop already." She swatted at him. "I mean, honestly. Your idea of fun was some old house that was on a television show from way back when. And a tea place."

"And you enjoyed both of them." He crossed his arms. "Admit it."

Her perfect lips pursed, but mirth glistened in her eyes.

"Anyway, I was thinking you need to see more of the mountains before you leave the area." *Good job, Benjamin. Keep reminding yourself she's not here to stay.*

"I can see them outside any windows in the area. I think I'm good."

"That's nothing compared to hiking in them. What if I took off a day and we ran over to Estes Park?"

A frown wrinkled her forehead. "Estes Park? That sounds like a place to skateboard or something."

"Nah. It's a cute little area a bit farther up in the Rockies. Lots of great trails near there. Some lakes. Shopping and eating. It's a great day trip."

"I love shopping." She tossed her hair over her shoulder. "But outdoors stuff is really not my thing. Didn't you hear me tell your sister that the other day?"

"I did, but I still think you just haven't experienced it the right way."

She shook her head.

"What's it going to take to prove to you I know how to have fun?" He plucked at his shorts. "I mean, I don't see how this isn't a blazing billboard for it."

"Okay. So maybe you're not completely dull." Her perfectly manicured finger tapped against her chin. "What if we do one of those random Walmart dates?"

"Date, huh?"

She waved a hand through the air. "That's just what it's called."

"How does it work?"

"You guys coming to eat, or not?" Alan hollered from the door. "No fun getting all dressed up like this and not showing off."

"We're coming." Benjamin's hand found the small of her back and guided her toward the door. Even though she stiffened at his first touch, she relaxed again quickly. Everyone else had already gone out and gotten into cars. How had they missed that?

As he steered his truck behind Keegan's SUV, he picked up their earlier conversation. "So? What's the random store date idea? Like what we did tonight?"

"Nope." She stared off at the mountains. "But it was a stupid idea. Forget I said it."

"How about this? I'll agree to do that one evening if you'll agree to spend a day in the mountains with me."

Her nose wrinkled. "Why is this so important to you?"

"I guess I can't help but want to share my love of God's

creation with everyone who comes around." He parked outside a local Mexican restaurant that was a favorite among their group. "Think about it over dinner, and let me know."

She didn't answer, but that was okay. Because it would take all his willpower to work up the self-esteem needed to walk into the eatery wearing this. And he'd discovered if he didn't push her into things, she usually came around to them anyway.

Even though she'd said it wasn't actually a *date*, something told him it would be marked in his memory as one. And he'd be a willing participant, even if it had him ending up in another crazy outfit. Because it meant time with her.

A dangerous game indeed. Because, as far as he could tell, she wasn't changing her mind on any of the resolutions she'd brought with her to Boulder.

10

Parked in front of the restaurant, every single one of Benjamin's limbs froze. Try as he might to blow this off as 'all in good fun,' the actuality of leaving this vehicle wearing this outfit had him frozen.

"Are you not hungry?" Skye broke through part of his haze of embarrassment.

"I am."

"You know the food is in there, right?" Her slender finger pointed toward the eatery.

"Yeah." A giant sigh escaped him. "But the drive-thru sounds very appealing right now."

"Surely you're not turning chicken now that you've proven your legs aren't related to the bird!"

"Of course not." He checked to make sure his collar was still popped right. "Just trying to protect you."

"Mm-hmm." Her voice held more skepticism than he appreciated.

"Okay. Let's do this thing." Before he could change his mind, he shoved the door open and climbed out of his truck, marching around to her side to help her out. A warm breeze swept by, caressing parts of his legs not usually exposed. Had his shorts shrunk in the hot vehicle?

He tugged at their hems and sent up an urgent prayer that no one outside of their insane group would be around to see him like this. Why hadn't that possibility crossed his mind before he decided this was a great idea? Had his desire to find excuses to spend time with Skye impeded his judgment more than he thought?

They stopped right inside the door, the rest of their group milling in the tiny entryway as servers scurried back and forth, pushing tables together and rearranging silverware.

"Did we not call ahead?" Alan asked the question to no one in particular.

Presley evidently overheard him, though. "We did, but they have some strange policy about not actually getting things ready until most of your group arrives. So here we wait."

"Wonder how many times they got burned by rearranging things only to have the people not show up and having to reset it all again." Benjamin stretched his neck, trying to work out the tension that had taken up residence there.

"I hadn't even considered that." Presley shot him an appreciative glance before turning back to another conversation.

Skye stepped closer—from jealousy? "It's crowded in here, huh?"

"A bit, I guess." He drew her arm through his. "Probably won't feel so tight when we're all seated instead of crammed in the entrance."

"True."

A quick surveillance of the room had his spine relaxing a bit. No one else in the restaurant seemed to notice their strangely clad group. The other customers were all focused on their food and the people in their own booths. Maybe crazy dressers came in here all the time.

"Looks like they're almost ready for us." Keegan waved from a few yards away.

"Sounds good."

Because of the congestion of people gathered, movement toward the table was slow. Since Benjamin and Skye were two of the last to come in, they were near the back. Adding to the sludge, several other tables had completed their meals about the same time their group started moving in, and the finished diners worked their way out through the middle of the inward flow.

Skye shook her head. "Good thing I had a late afternoon snack."

"Well, I didn't, and if I don't get to eat soon, I may have to eat this hat. Which would be a shame."

"It does look nice. Best find of the night, if I do say so myself." Skye buffed her fingers against her jacket.

"Agreed."

Finally the people blocking their way moved, and Benjamin and Skye snaked their way through the crowded room and toward the table where their friends were settling. As they passed the first booth, though, the man who had been sitting there stood and knocked into Benjamin. Benjamin quickly clasped the man's arm to keep them both from tumbling and then looked up to apologize.

Any and all ability of speech died on his tongue. A lump the size of Texas settled in his middle, and he had trouble drawing a full breath despite knowledge that the air hadn't actually left the room.

The raised eyebrow on the face in front of him was more than a little familiar. He saw it five days a week in the office where they both worked. Except Leon Marston was one of the senior attorneys, and Benjamin was still working his way up from lowly junior.

"Smith." Was that mirth or shock in Marston's eyes?

"Sir." Benjamin quickly released his hold on the senior partner.

"How about we swap?"

"Sir?" Benjamin inwardly cringed at the repeat of the same word. His vocabulary was normally much broader than this.

"I'll introduce to you my date if you introduce me to yours." A genuine smile stretched across the older gentleman's face.

"Oh!" Benjamin straightened. "Yes, sir."

A bit of air returned to his parched lungs as he glanced at the girl still holding on to his arm. And then he realized he'd inadvertently squeezed her to him when he froze from embarrassment. He quickly loosened his grip on her and shot what he hoped was an apologetic smile.

"Mr. Marston, this is Skye Jones, a friend. We're here with a group from church." Benjamin pulled at his collar, though it wasn't anywhere close to choking him. "And Skye, this is one of the senior attorneys at the firm where I work. Mr. Leon Marston."

"A pleasure." Marston clasped Skye's hand and gave almost a little bow. "And allow me to introduce you both to my wife, May. May, this is Benjamin Smith, the junior attorney who started with us two years ago."

May beamed a warm grin at both of them. "I've never seen such interesting outfits."

"Oh, um ..." He was at a complete loss. Any explanation seemed rather illogical and wasteful at this point.

"It's really a silly thing we're doing. Just for fun." Skye flipped her hair over her shoulder. "We started the evening at the local thrift store, picking out funny things for each other to wear. It supports the charity the store runs and gives us all a good laugh."

"What an interesting concept." May took in all the others seated a few tables away. "And quite the outcome of attire."

"Yes. This isn't normally the way I dress." If Benjamin's cheeks were as red as they felt, they clashed madly with his swim trunks.

"I can vouch for that." Skye giggled. "Though I told him the hat needed to stay. I'd love to see it with his usual bowtie."

He hadn't thought his cheeks could get any warmer …

"I agree wholeheartedly, dear." May patted Skye's hand. "Well, dinner was lovely, and we'll let you two get to yours. It was so nice to meet you both."

"See you tomorrow morning, Smith." Marston nodded before escorting his wife toward the exit.

A breath that must have held every ounce of air remaining in his body whooshed out. Had Marston thought him an idiot? Someone not professional enough to be part of their firm? Granted, there were three senior attorneys who made such decisions, but he was very influential and one of the original two.

"Hey. I thought you were hungry." Skye tugged him toward their group.

"I was."

"I bet you will be again once we see all the food choices. Come on."

Somehow he made it into his seat and focused on the menu long enough to pick something he normally liked. But his mind couldn't focus on any of the conversations happening around him. Not even the few times Skye tried to get him to join in helped. And normally she was the center of his attention.

All he could do was worry what the next morning might

bring. And wonder why on earth this had sounded like a good idea.

————————

Where had he gone? Sure, his body was still seated next to her, with his all-too-distracting hat and perfectly popped collar. But Benjamin had mentally gone somewhere else after running into his boss.

Why?

The meeting had been nothing but pleasant. Simple introductions and small talk for only a few minutes. But it seemed to have paralyzed him.

She wasn't the only one who noticed. Several of the others at the table shot him worried glances as the meal progressed. He ate well enough, but not like he had the other times they'd been together.

"What happened to Benjamin?" The boy on her other side —Reese? Sloan? Keegan?—motioned toward him and frowned.

"I'm not sure." She pitched her voice low, though Benjamin probably wouldn't notice even if she spoke at full volume. "I think it may have something to do with us running into one of his bosses a little while ago. But I didn't think anything went badly in that conversation, so I don't know."

"Huh."

When he'd suggested this outing, she'd been all for it. It was right up her alley. And the outfits hadn't turned out nearly as wild as they could have.

Benjamin had come across as being all in too. But the way he acted now, she wondered if he really was as comfortable as he'd come across when he'd posed after first exiting the bathroom.

It was just a silly little activity. And no one else seemed to be bothered by their over-the-top attire. So why was he? What had changed?

Was he so worried about his job? Had the boss said something she missed? Because she hadn't noticed anything odd about the conversation. Definitely nothing to cause concern.

But if he didn't snap out of it, she might need to find a way to put more distance between the two of them sooner rather than later. Because she had no desire to hang out with someone—friend or otherwise—who was so wrapped up in his career that he was afraid of being caught having harmless fun.

She dipped one last chip in the bowl of salsa between her and Benjamin and then sat back, stuffed full of chalupas, beans, and rice. The meal had been scrumptious, but the flavor was dulled by the mannequin of a man seated beside her. He didn't even fight her when she grabbed the check to pay for her own meal, something he'd never allowed before.

"Ready to go?" She poked his arm as he put his wallet back in his pocket.

"What?" He focused on her for the first time in almost an hour. "Oh! I didn't pay for your—"

"I got it." She waved him off. "But we're leaving. I asked if you were ready."

He glanced around. "Of course. Sorry."

Once again, they were the caboose of their flamboyant group. But he walked as quickly as possible, as if afraid lingering might have him running into more coworkers. His side glances around the room supported that theory.

"I wasn't a very good companion tonight, huh?" He held her door open while she slid in.

She waited until he'd walked around and started the truck before replying. "You've definitely been a better conversationalist the other times we were together. But everyone is allowed to have an off night, I guess."

"I must seem fickle. I mean, I was the one who suggested we come to this."

"And then you freaked out?"

"That's as good a way to put it as any."

They were quiet the rest of the way back to the church building. She didn't even wait for him to open her door, but shoved her shoulder against the stubborn thing and climbed out before he could play the gentleman. He took his hat off and ran his fingers through his hair while watching others wander toward the courtyard, where the firepit glowed.

"You still want to stay?"

"That was the plan." Her arms crossed over her chest, she planted her feet. Was he seriously wanting to skip the devotional part of the evening? If yes, then his rapid descent in her opinion had just picked up speed.

"Of course." He turned toward the rest of the group and moved like a zombie in that direction.

She blinked a few times. The smoke must have traveled across the parking lot already to make her eyes water like this. Nothing else could cause it, surely.

"Everything okay?" One of the other girls caught up with Skye before they reached the rest of the group. "I'm Samantha, by the way."

"Hey. Yeah. I guess." Her gaze trailed to Benjamin, who had slumped onto a bench at the edge of the courtyard.

"He's not usually like that. We're all a little worried. I guess I hoped he said something to you."

"No. Nothing."

"Hopefully he'll snap out of it soon and get back to his normal sweet self. All the girls here were amazed when we heard he was bringing someone tonight. No one has been able to catch his eye in years. We couldn't wait to see the special girl who did."

"Oh, no." Skye shook her head. "We're just friends."

"Tell yourself whatever you need to, but we've all seen the way he looks at you." Samantha gave Skye's shoulder a squeeze and then joined a group passing out marshmallows.

They were just seeing things, right? Because he didn't look at her any differently than anyone else.

Right?

He turned and scanned the area until his eyes met hers. A half-grin graced his lips and her feet moved of their own accord. What was she doing?

Had Rain been right? Was she accidentally playing with his heart? She tried so hard to not be a heartbreaker.

This was nothing but one of her FLIRTS, right?

"Hey. Wondered where you'd gone."

She lowered herself beside him. "Samantha caught me in the parking lot."

"She wanted to take your picture, right?"

A laugh escaped at the disgust in his voice. "No. Just girl talk. Introduced herself again."

"Girl talk. Like clothes ... or guys?"

Something fluttered up from her middle, but she willed it back under submission. "Well, since it's girl talk, I guess you'll never know."

"Too bad. I might have been interested in that conversation."

"There's a first time for all things tonight, it seems. You haven't been interested in much since we got to the restaurant." She clasped her hands between her knees.

"I'm sorry." He reached over and covered her fingers with his.

"Let's go ahead and worship for a little while and then we

can stuff the tiny little spaces left in our bellies full of these marshmallows." Keegan waved a Bible in the air. "Any guy who has a song to lead, just jump in whenever there's a pause. We'll sing for a little while, and then I have a few verses I think appropriate."

Benjamin's fingers remained where they were while they lifted voices in song. He had a wonderful bass voice, and she had to keep from staring at him each time he went lower. And when he started one of her favorite songs during a break, something large plopped in her middle, as if ice were melting.

"Okay, guys. Here's what I'm thinking goes well with our excursion tonight. When God decides King Saul isn't going to be king of Israel anymore, He sends Samuel to Jesse's family to anoint a new guy. Samuel keeps looking at the brothers, thinking he's found the right one. And what does God say?"

"Keep looking!" another guy called out.

Keegan pointed his Bible that direction. "That's right! He states that even though man looks at outward appearances, God looks at the heart."

Several chuckles went around the group, but Benjamin squirmed, his hand slipping off hers. Was he embarrassed about his earlier reaction? Or was it something else?

"Not that we aren't a handsomely attired group of people tonight." Keegan's laugh was catching. "But still, I've got to admit it was a little awkward to go out among others dressed this way. The good news for me was that I remembered my devotional thought. You all weren't privy to it yet."

More laughter.

"Well, not only does God care more about our hearts than our outsides, He also calls us to be different from the world. In Romans twelve, He says, 'Don't be conformed to this world, but be transformed by the renewal of your mind.' Maybe tonight can be a good reminder to us to stand out and not blend in with those around us. Though maybe not quite in this way again, huh?"

Keegan wrapped up his talk quickly, enforcing the reminders to work more on their insides than outsides and to be different. It wasn't anything deep, but it did a good job of weaving the evening together. After one more song and a prayer, most made their way toward the s'mores ingredients on the other side of the courtyard.

"Did you want some dessert?" Benjamin broke the silence on their bench.

"I'm still pretty full. Even if marshmallows are mostly air."

"True."

"Everyone gather in for a photo before you leave." Samantha stood on a bench nearby and waved her camera around.

"Maybe we could slip away and no one would notice." Benjamin motioned toward the parking lot.

"My clothes are still inside. Besides, we might as well document this stylish attire." She wove her fingers through his and dragged him over to the rest of the group.

He stood behind her, but she ducked enough that at least his head and hat would show. He might not be happy with how the evening had turned out, but it didn't mean she had to quit having fun. Something she needed to remember more.

Along with remembering to spend less time with him.

11

"I didn't know people still did these things at weddings." Skye tied a tiny piece of pink ribbon around a circle of tulle, wrapping up a clear cup full of bird seed. Her fiftieth to do in the last hour.

"Well, now you know." Rain set another box of cups next to her. "Aren't you glad that this bride only wants a hundred and fifty? The one next week wants five hundred paper cones full of flower petals."

Skye wrinkled her nose. "Does that mean they're expecting five hundred guests?"

"*At least* five hundred. Some people always leave early." Rain scooped more bird seed into the new cups. "You never did say how last night went."

"It went okay." If Skye focused on making a perfect bow of the extra-thin ribbon, she wouldn't have to meet her sister's eyes.

"Just okay? You sounded really excited about it before going."

"Well, let's just say I'm beginning to think maybe you were right about me spending too much time with Benjamin."

"Oh?" Rain's hands stilled.

"Yeah. I thought he was really excited about last night, too, but then once we were dressed up and at the restaurant, it was like he changed into a completely different guy. Especially after he ran into one of his bosses. I didn't think it was that big of a deal, but he sort of froze up and acted like a zombie or something the rest of the evening." Skye tossed another sachet in the fancy basket.

"It would be embarrassing to run into a senior attorney dressed like you guys probably were. I saw what you were wearing, but what did you end up putting him in?"

Skye's lips twitched. "Short red swim trunks, a grotesquely flowered Hawaiian shirt, and a pinstripe fedora."

Rain's laugh filled the small shop. "Oh, man. I need to get ahold of some pictures. I'm sure Samantha got quite a few."

"I know she got at least one of the whole group."

"I'll have to hit her up on Sunday." Rain handed her another cup of bird seed. "You don't want to spend time with him anymore because he was embarrassed?"

"I don't know. It was more like a confirmation that he's too serious about his job and that's not the type of guy I want to end up with. I've already lived with a guy like that, and I know what happens."

"What?" Rain stopped working and stared straight at Skye.

"Father let his work take over his life and never had any time for us after Mom died. I don't want to keep living like that. If I ever decided to get serious with a guy, I would want to make sure he's one who can find a balance."

Skye shrugged. "Besides, I'm only here for the summer, and everyone seems to be linking us together as more than friends.

I'm not ready for anything like that right now. I have too much else to figure out."

"Hmm." Rain's reply was noncommittal, though a contemplative look crossed her face.

That was fine with Skye. She didn't want to get into another argument with her sister. Especially since the last time, Rain called Benjamin to come find her.

"No plans for tonight, huh?"

"Just hanging out with my amazing sister and brother-in-law." The tulle felt scratchier with every sachet Skye tied. Who came up with such insane ideas?

"Hate to ruin those plans, but Jeremiah and I are going out tonight." Rain tied a perfect bow as if it were the easiest thing in the world.

"You are?"

"Big plans." Her sister chuckled. "Starting with the baseball dinner Jeremiah's team is having and then escaping early to make it to the rehearsal for this weekend's wedding. I think Jeremiah's hoping there will still be some cake left. They're having death by chocolate at the dinner tonight."

"So, basically, you're having a working date?" Skye wrinkled her nose. "That doesn't sound fun at all."

Rain tilted her head. "I mean, I get to spend time with my favorite guy. And we each get to support the other in the things we love—his sports and my events. Sounds pretty perfect to me. Especially if he treats me to coffee on the way home."

"Such high standards for a date night."

"We can't *all* go crazy and wear silly things from a thrift store to a public restaurant. Some of us enjoy having regular dates instead." Rain handed her another cup of seeds. "You rethinking your plans to stay home by yourself? Maybe Benjamin is having a better day today and won't be so zombie-like."

"There is a next-to-zero chance I will see Benjamin tonight." Skye rubbed her fingers together where they were hurting from the rough material.

"Oh really? Is that something you're taking bets on?"

"I'm not really a betting kind of girl, but even if I were, I'd still say the odds are in my favor."

Rain raised an eyebrow. "I'm going to make a wager."

"Seriously?"

"Yep. If you don't see Benjamin tonight, you can plan Jeremiah's and my next date. As long as there's nothing like skydiving."

"How is that a win for me? Sounds more like a win for you."

"Because you're always talking about how boring we are. You get to show us what you consider exciting."

"I'm still not sold."

"Fine." Rain pursed her lips. "And you won't have to help make those five hundred paper cones next week for the flower petals."

Skye leaned back and crossed her arms. "O-kay. And if I do, somehow, see Benjamin tonight even though I've already told you I won't?"

"Then, you have to be in charge of the flower girl at the wedding tomorrow."

"Ugh!" Skye jumped up and planted her fists on her hips. "There's incentive to stay home and have a boring evening if ever I heard one. I saw that little beast last week when they came in to get her dress. Never have I ever seen someone more spoiled."

"Exactly. But I still think I'm going to win this one."

"That's not a fair wager, regardless. That beast is much worse than five hundred paper cones."

"You haven't tried to make one yet." Rain tied up another sachet.

"You can't be serious. This is ridiculous. I'm not going to see Benjamin tonight. Why are we even talking about this?"

"You scared?"

Skye ground her fists deeper into her waist.

Rain raised an eyebrow.

The tip of Skye's bright pink ballet flat beat out a staccato rhythm.

Rain's lips smirked before she let out a "Bawk, bawk!"

"Fine. But I'm winning." Skye spun and marched toward the bathroom for a break from tulle ... and her sister.

"We'll see, sister dear. We'll see."

"Smith."

Here it came. Benjamin's feet halted where he'd been headed past Marston's door the next afternoon. Instead, he leaned against the frame and tried to meet his superior's gaze.

"Yes, sir."

"Doing okay today?"

"Yes, sir." Benjamin waved a stack of papers he'd just grabbed from the printer. "Just working on a simple will for the Henleys coming in next week."

"Good, good." Marston nodded and tapped a pen against his desk. "My wife enjoyed meeting you and your girl last night. Was really impressed."

"Oh, um, thank you, sir. But we're just friends."

"Mm." Marston gave a curt nod. "I was young once, too, you know. I've seen friendships like that turn into something else."

"I don't know. I mean, Skye is ..."

"Yes. May was once too." Marston winked. "And we just celebrated forty years together a few weeks ago."

Forty years. The idea of that long with Skye intrigued and exhausted him. But it was a moot point. She continuously reminded him she wasn't the marrying kind.

Benjamin rubbed the back of his neck. "Well, I may have messed things up a bit last night, so it's probably too late for that one."

"Don't tell me it was because of me." Marston straightened in his chair.

"Oh—" And how did he answer that? It wasn't, really. And yet, if he hadn't run into him in that getup, would Benjamin have had a better reaction?

"I hope you weren't embarrassed about your outfit. I never did anything exactly like that, but I have worn worse. In public." Marston chuckled. "I think some of those clothes were from back in the day when I was in a bit better shape. I remember being quite the stud in some swim trunks like those red ones you had on."

Why did Benjamin insist on keeping his face clean shaven? It only showed off more the pink that had to be creeping up his cheeks at the moment. He'd never expected such a statement from the gentleman who'd been his mentor the last few years.

"Now, don't let that girl get away. If she really is like my May, she's worth doing everything you can to keep her." Marston winked again. "Though I'm glad to see you traded that shirt from last night for your normal attire today."

"Yes, sir." Benjamin gulped.

"Go on, then. Don't let me keep you with my reminiscing." Marston waved him off as he turned to answer his now-ringing phone.

As if shackles had been removed, his step was lighter as he crossed the hallway to his office. Forty years. He slid into his seat. But would she even see him again, to say nothing of wanting more?

Only one way to find out. It didn't take him but a second to start a new text message.

What ya doing?

He set his phone aside. No use sitting and waiting for who-knew-how-long it might take her to respond. Not that his eyes agreed with that decision. They kept sneaking peeks at the screen to see if anything new had popped up.

Benjamin finished the prep for Tuesday's will signing and moved on to working on some property transfer paperwork before a chime came from his device. Forty-five minutes. Had she been busy, or was she trying to come up with an excuse not to answer?

Sliding the phone his way, he swiped across to open the message.

Removing the shoulder pads from a blazer someone bought me. Thought I might be able to make it more palatable that way.

He smirked.

Oh yeah? How's that working out for you?

Not so well, actually, but I don't give up easily.

That could be taken many different ways. His thumbs hovered over the keypad as he tried to decide the best way to phrase his next question. Only half an hour until quitting time, so he needed to figure this out quickly.

Those all your plans for tonight?

Three bouncing dots appeared and then disappeared again.

What had she been about to say? It happened again. And a third time. He hadn't considered his question to be that difficult. While waiting for a response, he cleared out his inbox and straightened things on his desk.

Doesn't that sound like a fun Friday night?

Seriously? This from the girl who wanted everything to be an adventure? Something fishy was going on.

Not particularly. But I've never removed shoulder pads before.

Ha!

Nothing else. Fifteen minutes until time to leave.

Tell me more about the store date idea. I'm needing more excitement on my Friday night.

Three dots, and then they disappeared again. Had he actually ruined any chances he had with this woman over a stupid moment of embarrassment the night before?

"Have a good evening, Smith." Marston rapped on his doorframe before waving and heading down the hall.

"You too, sir!"

He'd have a better idea of how his evening would go if he could get an actual reply from Skye. But she was acting more standoffish than when they'd first met. It seemed whatever headway he'd made over the last few weeks was ruined by the stupid outing the night before.

You can't do the store date with only one person. It has to be two.

Okay. So, let me pick you up, and you can show me.

No response. The clock turned over to five. He shut things down and grabbed his briefcase. Now what?

Maybe another time.

His heart sank. So much for that idea. He replied with a gif of a cartoon character crying his eyes out. It's all he had left.

As he climbed in his truck, his phone beeped again.

Oh, good grief. Fine. Come on. But you owe me.

And what was that supposed to mean? It didn't matter. He'd figure it out when he got there.

Running home to change clothes and then I'll pick you up.

K.

What was he heading into? Too late now. He'd talked her into it, and he wasn't about to waste the opportunity.

12

Skye slid into Benjamin's passenger seat as if it were the most natural thing in the world. And maybe it was. He couldn't find a reason to complain—except for maybe the frown marring her normally perfect face.

"You okay?"

"Fine."

He left the truck in park and just studied her. "No more explanation about that text saying I owe you?"

Her lips twitched, but she shook her head. "Nope."

When she still wouldn't give him anything else after another couple minutes, he gave up and headed out of Rain's driveway. "So, I'm saving you from a boring night of shoulder pad surgery, huh?"

She snickered. "It's not like there was much else going on. The sappy movie channel is already showing Christmas movies, for some reason. I mean, it's the end of June!"

"Wait, wait, wait. You mean to tell me that the girl who always wants to think outside the box and do exciting things thinks Christmas should be kept to a certain time of year?"

"Celebrating a holiday all year long isn't exciting. It becomes mundane." Skye brushed something off her jeans. "I'm not against mixing things up and thinking outside the box, but really people have just put Christmas in two boxes instead of one—the regular Christmastime slot, and July."

"I guess I can see that." He drummed his fingers on the steering wheel. "And Rain and Jeremiah didn't have anything else exciting you could join in?"

"They're doing some work-date thing with his baseball team and then her rehearsal for tomorrow's wedding." She shook her head as if it were the saddest thing she'd ever heard. "I was rather glad to not be invited."

"Where are we going for this random store date?"

"Oh, just a normal store. Walmart is probably best."

"Walmart it is. And what exactly are we doing? Are you finally going to let me in on this amazing idea?" He shot a glance her way. "Please tell me there are no crazy clothes involved."

A huff escaped her mouth. "No, there is no need for you to go back into your crazy, zombie mannequin, freak-out phase you were in last night. No crazy clothes involved."

"I wasn't a ... did you say zombie mannequin?"

"It's the best description I could come up with." Her slender fingers tapped out a rhythm on her leg.

"Listen, I'm sorry about last night." He ran a hand through his hair. "I know I didn't handle things well. All I could think of was that Mr. Marston might decide I wasn't serious enough to keep my position once he saw me dressed like that. It had nothing to do with you. I've just worked so hard to get to the point I'm at in the firm ..."

"Let's just make a deal, okay?" Skye turned more toward him. "No more talk about last night or work."

His mouth hung open for several seconds before he gave a

curt nod and slammed it closed. "Got it. We're here. What's the plan?"

"It's pretty easy." She accepted his help down from her seat. "Basically, we go down aisles like snack foods or frozen stuff or drinks to get everything for our date night. We can also check out movies or games or something."

"And we just pick what we want?"

"Nope. That's where the challenge comes in. One of us will go down the aisle until the other yells, 'Stop!' and then the first person has to pick something off the shelf right in front of them. Even if your favorite cookies are farther down."

"Hmm." He grabbed a shopping cart. "Okay. So we'll need food and entertainment. Anything else?"

"I think that's enough for this time, isn't it?"

"The only other thing I could think of was maybe slippers or a blanket to watch the movie under."

She giggled. "Let's see how the rest goes first before we decide to add to it."

"Got it. Where should we start?" Walmart on a Friday was overwhelming for him on a normal basis. Adding in this extra pressure had his brain spinning without traction.

"Maybe entertainment? That way if we get something frozen, it won't have too much time to melt."

"Makes sense. Games? Movies?"

"Are you a game player?"

"I get pretty fierce when challenged with a board and a little metal figure to move around." He flashed her a grin, and she replied with one of her own.

"Let's go then." She led the way to the toy section and stood at the edge. "You want to be the picker or should I start?"

"Show me how it's done. I just tell you when to stop?" He craned his neck to try and see where certain games were located, but this section was a bit chaotic and jampacked.

"You got it. Here I go."

When she was about halfway down, just at the border of the cards section and board games, he told her to stop. Her finger pointed as her eyes scanned different titles and types. Just when he'd been about to suggest she move down a foot, she grabbed a red box and brought it back to put in the cart.

"What is it?"

"Some sort of game where you have to guess what word the other person thinks fits a description best. Sounded funny."

"You think we know each other well enough to be able to play something like that?"

"Guess we'll find out." She pushed the cart back out into the main aisle. "Ready to head toward the food?"

"Lead the way."

About halfway around the back of the store, a big bin was full of marked-down DVDs. "Skye, wait. Want to grab one of these in case we get tired of the game?"

"All right." She tilted her head and studied the display before nodding. "You start digging, and I'll say when. Whatever you're holding is the one we take."

"Unless it's rated R."

"Okay. Unless that." She motioned him to start.

He reached his hand in as deep as he could, not sure about this plan. The caliber of films normally available in these sections wasn't always stellar. But he let his hand slide over various cases until she told him to stop. Holding his breath, he lifted the choice. And laughed.

A Christmas movie from the '90s.

She covered her face with her hands, but her shoulders shook with her giggles. "I give up! It was obviously meant to be. Let's go get some food and get out of here."

"Deal."

On the drink aisle, they ended up with a bottle of strawberry soda and a root beer. In one frozen section he got to choose and picked a mac and cheese meal and some pizza bites. She grabbed a pack of popcorn and chocolate caramels. He snatched a box of sundae cones.

"What else?" He surveyed the crazy collection in the cart.

Tapping her finger on her chin, she joined his appraisal. "I'm not sure. Can you think of anything else we need?"

"I think this is great. And if we find we need something else, I'm sure there's something in the kitchen."

"Fair enough. Let's go."

He waved her off as she offered to help pay, and they made their way out of the store with their bags of goodies. "Okay. Back to Rain's place or mine?"

"If Rain saw all this junk food in her house, she'd have a conniption. Not that she didn't used to eat this way, but she's gone healthier since moving out here."

"Nothing wrong with eating junk food every now and then. It's all about moderation." He set the bags at her feet and slid in behind the wheel. "That's why I grabbed the mac and cheese with cauliflower."

"You didn't!" She froze with her seatbelt halfway buckled.

"I did. It's yummy."

There went that frown again.

He shook his head and tutted. "Pretty sure you have to at least try a bite. Isn't that part of the fun of this type of thing?"

"It might be if it didn't include yucky cauliflower." Her pert little nose wrinkled up.

"You won't even notice it because it blends in with the noodles and cheese."

"I'm just not believing you."

"Well, I'll have to prove you wrong, then." He steered them

toward his townhouse. "You gonna tell me more about why you said I owe you now?"

<hr>

"Nope." Why, oh why, had she typed that stupid message earlier? Hoping he'd back out of his insistence on them doing this so she wouldn't lose her silly little bet with Rain?

And there was a bigger why. Why had she agreed to such a ridiculous scheme to begin with? She'd been so sure she'd be able to turn Benjamin down should he contact her—not that she'd actually expected him to after last night. But then those stupid movies held no appeal. And the cupboards were full of healthy stuff that sounded gross. And boredom had won the bet for Rain.

Not that she'd totally gotten out of eating healthy stuff. Cauliflower!

"Here we are." Benjamin pulled her from her regrets, and she looked up at a brick exterior.

Through the living room, she followed with one of the bags. His space was neat, which fit her mental image of him. A few paintings on the wall, mostly landscapes. Family photos lined the streamlined mantel. A small kitchen filled the back corner of the living area, and they set their bags on the counters together.

"Let's get some of this heating up, and then we can eat."

"I call starting with dessert."

"Now who's being a chicken?" He smirked as he waved the cardboard container of contaminated macaroni her direction. "I dare you."

"Do I look like the kind of girl who takes dares?" Had she ever said anything more ridiculous? Of course, she was.

"You really want me to answer that?"

"Oh, just heat up the stuff!" She stashed the ice cream in the freezer—also organized and neat. Just as predictable as she'd originally thought. Though she'd been considering him less so lately.

In his living room she gathered some throw pillows off the couch and moved them to the rug by the coffee table. Cozy as she could make it.

"What are you doing?" He brought in paper plates and napkins. "The pizza bites and macaroni are heating."

"I just figured we could try to play the game while we eat." She flopped down on a cushion.

"And we can't sit on the actual furniture because ...?"

"It's more fun to eat on the floor."

He shook his head, but the corner of his mouth tilted up before he turned back toward the kitchen. She'd take it.

She skimmed the rules of the game while he banged around in the kitchen. More noise than she'd expect from food that was mostly automatic. Various scents wafted her way, including buttery popcorn. Her tummy sent out a welcome growl as he placed the bowl beside her.

"Come fix a plate." He held out his hand and gave a tug to help her up.

"Thanks."

The pizza bites were easy to pile on, but she hesitated at the other dish. It looked safe enough, but just knowing what was inside ...

"Close your eyes."

"What?" Her head jerked his way.

"Close your eyes." He waved a fork her direction. "And open your mouth."

The battle waging war inside her was fierce. Every other time he'd convinced her to try a new food, it had turned out well. But that was different. The hurt crossing his face the longer she hesitated turned the tide, though. She sighed and followed his command.

A moment later, warm gooiness crossed her lips and landed on her tongue. Creamy. Salty. Cheesy. She let her lips close around it and savored it before exploring the texture. Not as awful as she'd expected, though it definitely wasn't normal.

"Not as bad as you thought?"

"What do I get if I agree?" Her eyes slowly opened and discovered him standing much closer than she'd expected. She jerked backward and banged into the counter.

"More yummy mac and cheese?" He turned toward his own plate as if she hadn't just overreacted to his proximity.

"Fine."

Plates piled with food, they settled on the floor. He grabbed her hand before she could take another bite and bowed his head. Right.

"Father God, thank you for this friendship you've given us this summer. Thank you for the time we have to spend together and for the fun ideas Skye comes up with. Help us be a blessing to each other and others. Amen."

They ate in silence for a few moments. The pasta did leave a slight aftertaste Skye wasn't used to, but she washed it down with her strawberry soda. He motioned toward the game, and she explained the rules as best she could understand them.

It only took a few rounds before it was obvious this game wasn't going to work with only the two of them.

"Are you serious? You think Hoover Dam is a great term to match up with *leaky*?" Skye threw his card back at him. "Oh, my goodness! I think there's a reason this is recommended for more than two players."

He snorted his root beer. "Probably. Should we try the movie instead?"

"Only if we can bring in the sweets to go with it."

"You go grab those, and I'll start this classic."

She dumped the last few bites of her macaroni and dug the ice cream out of the freezer. The first few notes of "I'll Be Home for Christmas" played from the television as she plopped back down with the treats.

"We're really going to do this?" She stuffed a handful of chocolate caramels in her mouth.

"Of course. How can you not like this? His whole goal in life is to get back to his family for Christmas, and nothing is going right along the way. It was the feel-good story of whatever year it first released."

"Mm. I'm beginning to think we don't agree on TV and movies."

"I bet it wins you over before the end."

She settled back against the couch and leaned her head on his shoulder. "And to think I agreed to spend this evening with you so I wouldn't have to watch a Christmas movie."

"Win-win." He crunched into his ice cream cone. "Speaking of which, I believe you said something about you'd go hiking with me if I did this store date with you."

A groan escaped her before she could stop it. How had she forgotten that agreement? Because she'd been too wrapped up in the angst of losing her sister's wager? Although the reminder of her sister gave her a bit of an out.

"I'm sort of booked for the foreseeable future. Weddings every weekend. I think Rain even has two scheduled next week. And one of those is massive."

"No Saturdays?"

"Right."

"What day during the week is the least busy at the shop?"

She leaned back so she could see his face. "What does it matter? You have to work too."

"I have days I can take. I haven't used much of my time off over the last few years."

"You'd actually skip a day of work just to take me on a hike?"

"It's called priorities. And you're becoming one."

No words. Nothing. Her heart teeter-tottered somewhere between terror and awe. She barely swallowed the bite of caramel lodged in the back of her throat.

"Oh, watch this scene." He pointed toward the screen. "It's really funny."

She gladly turned her focus back to the movie, though it didn't hold her attention. How could it after a statement like that? One that confirmed what she'd been fighting for weeks now, despite having it pointed out by several people.

By coming over here, she'd not only gotten herself deeper into this mess—she also now had to wrangle the flower girl of terror tomorrow. She squeezed her eyes shut and wished to wake up back at Rain's house, picking apart her silly blazer and watching a Christmas movie. But the pleasant scent of Benjamin's cologne and the cushion that wasn't as comfy as she'd claimed chained her to reality.

And reality grew more complicated every day she remained in Colorado.

13

"Of course, it isn't going to come out." Skye added a bit of hand soap to the paper towel she'd been using to dab the filmy satin of her dress. The red punch seemed to grow darker and spread farther instead of fading with the cleaning treatment of whatever the bathroom had to offer. Trying to wrangle a seven-year-old flower girl was one thing, but accepting that flower girl ruining one of Skye's best dresses was something else entirely.

A stall opened behind her, and the lady met Skye's glance in the mirror. "Let me guess. My lovely niece strikes again."

This woman was the first person all day Skye had heard not sound completely enamored with the brat, who insisted on being the star of the wedding. Still, better at least to try and not sound as upset as she was, just in case she misinterpreted the tone of voice. "The flower girl is your niece?"

"Yes. Let me just apologize for my family's poor choices in raising her. I don't want to excuse them, but I can explain a little." She finished washing her hands and grabbed some paper towels. "My sister is raising her as a single mom right now. Her husband's been deployed more often than not for much of Kaitlyn's life. It doesn't mean my sister shouldn't use more discipline, but I think she coddles and spoils her because she's trying to compensate for Brett not being around."

Skye shut the water off on her own sink. It wasn't doing any good on her garment anyway. The story hadn't won over much of her sympathy, either, but she should probably try to act like it had. "I guess I can understand that a little."

"Like I said, it doesn't excuse her from the fact she's let her daughter turn into a complete brat. And my parents seem only to help with that part." She rubbed her belly, obviously swollen with pregnancy. "It's why my husband and I put our foot down with the first of ours. We didn't want to follow her down that road."

"This is your second?" Skye motioned toward her belly.

"Oh, no. This is number four. I think my husband is aiming for a basketball team." She giggled and rubbed her bump as if she hadn't said something completely foreign to Skye. "I'm Abby, by the way. My other sister was the bride today. I'm the oldest."

"Nice to meet you." Skye accepted her handshake. "I'm the sister of the wedding planner."

"Hence the fun job of trying to control the flower girl." Abby nodded. "Well, don't let our family scare you. Not all marriages and families turn out as crazy as ours. And, to be honest, I think it's more fun to have them a little crazy."

"No offense, but I have no plans to settle down. Didn't even before today."

"That's a shame." She tutted. "Marriage is the best adventure I've ever been on."

"Adventure?" No way. She'd probably just chosen the wrong word in her pregnancy-brained haze.

"You bet." Abby grinned and paused by the bathroom door.

"I mean, it's not all the risky things we used to do like mountain climbing or ziplining. We've calmed a bit with each baby. But there are still lots of fun moments. And as each child comes along and starts experiencing all the things we already know about, it's awesome to see the joy of discovery in their eyes."

Skye's chest ached as the words sank in deep. "But isn't it more of the same-old, same-old, each and every day?"

"No way. I can't remember the last time I had a day that felt just like the one before it. Every day is different. Some bring more laughter, and others come with tears. But the best part of marriage is that I don't have to do it all alone. If I don't know what to do, he's right there to help me figure it out. Or, if it's something really good, it's even better because we can share it." Abby winked. "Keep that in mind."

She slipped through the door only to pop back in a second later. "And for the punch stain, try a bit of baking soda, peroxide, and blue dish soap. Make it a paste and test it on a part of your dress that won't show first. If it doesn't discolor, use it on the stain. It takes out almost everything. Trust me. I have three boys, with another on the way."

Skye blinked as the bride's sister disappeared once more. Her words reverberated in Skye's mind. And a big part of her longed to grasp onto the ones about having someone to help when she didn't know what to do.

A crash on the other side of the door jerked her back to the present. She'd been in here much too long. Time to go help Rain wrap up this disaster of a wedding.

Rain glanced up from where she swept up bits of glass, cake, and frosting smeared all over the floor around her. "There you are."

"Sorry. Was trying to keep this stain from setting in, but I don't think I had any more luck than whoever carried this mess." She knelt down and gathered a few of the bigger pieces in her hands. "Do I want to know what happened?"

Rain raised an eyebrow. "Guess."

"Bet it starts with the same letter as the person who stained my dress."

"*Ding, ding, ding.*"

The hotel staff came over with cleaning supplies and took over so Rain and Skye could blend into the background once more. Skye glanced around the room, her eyes landing on Abby with her brood of boys, all gathered around a table, laughing. Abby turned and said something to the man beside her, and he chuckled before pressing a kiss to her temple.

"You okay?" Rain's question pulled her back from the edge of something Skye wasn't sure she wanted to step over.

"Fine. It's just been a long afternoon."

"Thanks for all your help this summer. I know it isn't your job of choice, but you really have made things easier. This is my first year to have so many weddings booked, and it's proving I need to hire someone on full-time in the near future."

"Well, I'm glad I was some help, but I'm not interested even if that were an invitation."

"Just throwing it out there." Rain smirked. "Though it would keep you close to a certain attorney. You know—the one you weren't going to see last night."

Skye scowled. "I've paid my due. And it possibly cost me one of my favorite dresses to boot."

"I know, I know. I just couldn't resist. You looked so busted when you got home last night."

"All we did was eat dinner and watch a movie."

"Rather low-key for you, isn't it?"

"Well, we did make a game of picking out what we'd eat and watch." Skye shifted her weight, the back of her sandals pinching after wearing them for six hours straight so far.

"Of course, you did. Well, just a little longer here, and then we can let the cleaning crews take over and go soak in a bubble bath."

"And then do it all over again next week, right?"

"Two next week." Rain nodded. "I'm bringing in a few extra temporary helpers for those. And then the next weekend is Benjamin's sister's wedding. Did you ever make up your mind about being his plus one?"

"I don't think I was ever officially asked to be his plus one." Skye's gaze wandered back over to Abby's family once more. "Besides, I really do think I need to step back from that situation."

"Mm-hmm." Rain sounded anything but convinced.

"I thought you wanted me to back off." Skye struggled to gain control of her temper. "Didn't you warn me that he might not consider all this to be one of my FLIRTS? Well, I think you were right. And it doesn't need to go any further."

"I think you might be too late."

Before Skye could question her sister about that dire statement, Rain was whisked into the final events of the wedding. Mostly that consisted of moving all the guests out to the front drive so they could toss birdseed at the happy couple as they rushed away to their shaving-cream-covered car. Skye remained in the quiet room, gathering a few of the items she knew to be Rain's instead of those rented from the hotel.

The table where Abby's family sat had napkins covered with pen drawings of cars and dinosaurs and silly stick-figure families. Her fingers traced one with a man and woman and a baby. Adventure? It didn't fit the image in her head, but it hadn't looked nearly as boring across the ballroom as her past suppositions made it out to be.

Was she too late to back out of whatever this was with Benjamin in more than one way?

That couldn't be right.

Monday morning, Benjamin scanned his calendar for the rest of the week. Thursday was completely open. He could've sworn he had at least one appointment there at the end of last week.

"Fern, is Thursday really as free as it looks on my calendar?" Leaning on the countertop in front of the receptionist's desk, he waited while she pulled up his information on her screen.

"Oh, yes. I meant to send a note. The Andersons had to reschedule. Something about guests being able to visit for the first time in ten years. I had to shift them out a few weeks, but they didn't seem to mind."

"So, I literally have the whole day free on Thursday." He tapped a finger to his chin.

"Looks that way. Whatcha thinking?"

"I'm thinking I may take advantage of that. I've been promising a friend I'd take her up to see the Estes Park area. Maybe go for a hike."

"I haven't been up there in ages. It's a pretty area."

"It is." And he hadn't talked to Skye at all since dropping her back at Rain's house Friday night. That might have only been a few days, but it was getting to where he didn't want to go more than a few hours without having some sort of communication with her. "Is there anything else I need to be here for that day?"

"Let's see." She clicked a few more times, and ran her finger down the screen. "Some of the other attorneys have signings that day, but we have enough people around who can act as witnesses. You should be okay to go. Want me to mark you out?"

"Please, and thank you."

"You've got it. Soak it up for me. Who knows the next time I'll get a day off to go play like that." She smirked as she made a note in the computer. "And make sure you treat that *friend* of yours right. There's a sweet little restaurant before you get out of town. It has a view of the lake and the best soups and sandwiches."

"I'll be sure to keep it in mind. Thanks." He rapped on the desk before heading back to his office.

Now he just had to convince Skye that this was a good plan. Not to mention make sure Rain wouldn't need her that day. Probably something he should've done first.

Should he call Rain or Skye? If he asked Rain, Skye would probably be offended that he'd tried to arrange things behind her back. But if he simply asked Skye, she could tell him she had to work even if she didn't. Not that he thought she'd lie, but she hadn't acted normal since their date Friday.

When he'd seen her across the church auditorium Sunday, her glance had met his, and then she'd disappeared before he could work his way over to her. When he asked Rain about it, she'd answered in a manner that suggested she wasn't telling him everything. No. Something had happened Friday that had Skye going back to her standoffish self, and he wasn't about to let that ugly mask slip into place.

Ding.

He glanced at his phone screen. Amelia.

Rain picked up all the suits from the tailor. Can you get yours this week so she can mark that off the list?

Perfect.

I'm on it.

She sent him a happy emoji along with half a dozen others. He rolled his eyes and tucked his phone away. Time to get a bit more work done before five o'clock. Because he had an appointment to get to as soon as office hours were over.

> And don't forget you need to confirm your plus one.

Nothing like trying to kill two birds with one stone. Or convince them to agree to impossible things, as the case may be. Hiking *and* a wedding date? He might be pushing his luck this evening, but she'd never say, 'Yes,' if he never asked.

Okay, God. You know what my heart wants. And you know what she's said. Help a guy out here.

The last three hours of the day dragged by slower than the last quarter of a college football game. Benjamin didn't accomplish much work, his mind constantly forming possible scenarios and then squashing them with how they'd probably end up. He finally set aside the trusts he'd been working on and saved everything. Might as well give up two minutes early. He wasn't getting anything else done this day.

"Have a good one, Smith." Mr. Gaines waved as he headed out.

Benjamin closed things down and followed suit. Imaginary conversations with Skye would get him nowhere. Time to find out what she'd really say.

Less than half an hour later, he set the bells jingling over the door of Happily Ever After. Skye wasn't at her usual perch behind the counter. In fact, the place seemed quieter than normal. He took a few steps in and then heard a soft conversation going on behind the curtain that hid Rain's office space.

He flipped mindlessly through a bridal magazine while he waited, but it didn't hold his attention any better than anything else had that afternoon. When Rain stepped out, relief and disappointment warred within him. He'd hoped for Skye.

"Hey, Benjamin. Did Amelia send you?"

"She did." He rose and craned his neck to peek behind Rain as she let the curtain drop back in place, but he didn't notice any blonde hair hiding back there.

"Come with me, and we'll make sure it fits okay before I let you take it." She headed up the stairs. "Amelia caught a great deal on these suits. Since the tailor was selling off old stock, she paid way less buying them than renting. And you can have it for future uses."

"Sure." He squashed the gnawing growing in his middle. Officially he was here to get the suit. If he missed Skye this time, he'd just call her later.

"It's that time of day when we need a second wind, and Skye just stepped out to get us both a coffee." Rain pressed the wheat-colored suit into his hands. "Take your time trying this on."

He just caught a glimmer of mischief in her eye before she shut the door behind her. Okay, then. He still had hope.

No one was around when he opened the door, the new suit snug across his shoulders. A peek in the other open rooms upstairs also showed them to be empty. Down the stairs it was, then.

The moment his foot hit the bottom step, the door opened, and Skye blew in with a warm summer breeze. Her hair was in a long braid over her shoulder, and her bright pink capris shone under her sleeveless flowery top. She froze, her mouth open as her eyes took him in from head to toe.

"It's not my normal style." He brushed the lapels. "But my sister doesn't tend to listen to me when she asks my opinion."

Skye shook herself out of her stupor and moved to set the coffees on the counter. "No, it looks nice. No bowtie?"

"She wouldn't let me. Said it would look weird with all the others wearing these." He flicked his pink plaid tie before shoving his hands in his pockets. "But it's only for a few hours. And my cousin is allowing bowties, so there's that."

"I forgot you were in two weddings this summer."

"Yep." He stepped as close as he dared. "And for some reason, they both want me to have a date."

"I've never understood that. Since when is a wedding a date event? Isn't it supposed to just be about celebrating with friends and family? Who wants some stranger attending their wedding just so all the invited guests have dates?" Her hand knocked one of the coffee cups, and she dove to catch it before it spilled.

"Something about having an even number of place settings or something." He shrugged. "I'd love to have your company on those days. I know Rain will have you working during the wedding itself, which is sort of perfect since I'll be in the wedding party. But then you could hang out with me during the reception when the bride and groom don't need me."

"I don't know, Benjamin."

She hadn't met his eyes since that first moment walking in. Was she trying to avoid him for some reason?

"Well, that looks perfect." Rain came out from behind her curtain and nodded. "I know Amelia will be pleased. And since Chet is renting his, it won't be ready until right before the ceremony."

"Sounds good. I'm sure he'll let me know." Benjamin flashed Rain a smile. "I actually came with a double agenda today."

"Oh?" Rain's lips twitched as if amused.

"My calendar ended up completely empty on Thursday. And I mentioned to Skye the other day that Estes Park has some great hiking and views. I just needed to see if she'd be available to join me. I know it's close to the weekend and major wedding times, but I'm hoping maybe she could slip away for at least the morning."

Rain raised a brow. "It should be fine for her to get away until that afternoon when we'll need to be on hand for a wedding rehearsal. But it's up to her. I know hiking isn't usually her cup of tea. Though Estes Park is one of my favorite spots around here."

"But don't we need to make all those paper cones for the flower petals?" Skye widened her eyes at her sister.

"That's on the agenda for Wednesday, actually. Thursday is just final touches, and I can handle that. You should go. Who knows how many more opportunities you'll get to go see more of the mountains while you're here."

"It's up to you." Benjamin lowered his voice as he faced Skye. "But you did say if we did the crazy store date, you'd consider it."

Her blue eyes finally met his, and so many different emotions swirled in their depths, he couldn't begin to decipher what went through her head. "Fine."

"It'll be fun." He nodded, before backing a few steps away. "Guess I better go take this off again so it doesn't get dirty before Amelia's wedding. She'd kill me."

Skye nodded and then turned to her coffee. He glanced at Rain, who appeared concerned. Nothing made sense about this whole situation. Nothing except the fact that Skye had agreed to spend Thursday with him.

One step in the right direction? Or one step closer to falling off a mountain?

14

Skye was uncharacteristically quiet as Benjamin followed the road out of Boulder and up to Estes Park. It wasn't a hard drive, but it would take close to an hour to get to the small valley town at the doorstep of Rocky Mountain National Park. He planned to stop and catch the view for a moment before heading into the park for a few hikes. Then they could eat at the cute little café Fern had recommended on the way back.

That was the plan, anyway.

Skye stared out her window, saying nothing. Had he offended her somehow? If she hadn't wanted to come, why had she agreed? Had he been pushier than he meant to?

"Okay over there?" He tapped his fingers on the steering wheel in rhythm with the country song on his radio.

"Mm-hmm." She finally turned her pretty blue eyes his way.

"Glad to be away from work for a few hours?"

"Sure."

"I would've thought you'd jump at the chance to have an

adventure instead of prepping for a wedding." Nothing about today was typical. Should he just give up and turn around?

"I normally would." Her perfect brow wrinkled into a slight frown as if even she didn't understand why she wasn't acting like her usual self.

"Maybe it's just that you haven't caught sight of some of the pretty things we'll see today." He glanced her way once more. "I mean, besides your own reflection. Because you look very pretty today."

She shook her head, but a tiny grin lifted the corners of her lips. "It's just a T-shirt and some jeans."

"Well, it looks good on you." And it did. She might call it a normal T-shirt, but he could guarantee none of his fit like that, with little puckers in the sleeves and lace across the top of the back.

"If you say so." She scooted to face him a bit more. "What all are we supposed to be doing besides hiking?"

She said the last word as if it were sour.

"I picked a few pretty easy trails. One has a nice lake view at the end." He circled his finger in the air to indicate a circular shape. "We might see some fun animals. And I have a cute little restaurant picked out for lunch. Depending on when we get back to that, we might have a bit of time for some shopping, if you like. Then I plan to deliver you safely to your sister so she can put you back to work."

"So helpful."

The giant stone with "Estes Park" chiseled into it loomed ahead. He pulled into the little parking area beside it and motioned out to the view around them.

"This is it?" Skye sounded less than impressed.

"This is just the beginning of it. A good place to see some mountains and take a picture. We'll drive through in a minute, but I thought you'd like to see this."

"Sure."

Out of the car, motion at their feet had Skye hopping backward into his chest. A couple of chipmunks scurried across the rocks. Skye leaned down to get a closer look, her face a study of wonder and enchantment.

"I don't think I've ever seen a chipmunk before. Only squirrels in my yard in Missouri."

"We have squirrels, too, but these guys are pretty popular around here." He held up a finger. "Wait a second."

In his glove box, he unearthed an old granola bar and brought it back. "I bet we could give them a few nibbles."

"These are safe for them to eat?"

"Pretty sure they've been fed much worse." He chuckled and broke off half for her. "At least this has nuts in it."

Her giggles lifted his spirits as she watched the animals enjoying their snack. "They're so cute. When you mentioned seeing wildlife, I wasn't sure about it, but this I can handle."

"Good to know. Want to take our picture? Proof you visited more than Boulder?" He pointed toward the sign.

She nodded and posed beside him, her head tilted just right as he snapped their selfie. At least she was acting more like the fun, vivacious girl he'd liked more and more over the last few weeks. Maybe this day wouldn't be a bust after all.

Through the town of Estes Park, Skye's attention went back and forth as she took in everything. Then, a little farther on, they reached the entrance to Rocky Mountain National Park. Just before the toll booth, he pulled onto the shoulder and motioned toward a field on the right.

"Look over there."

Skye's nose practically pushed against his window. "What are they? Reindeer?"

"Elk."

"Really? I thought those lived somewhere else. Like Canada or something."

"There probably are some in Canada, too, but there are a ton around here." He leaned over and rolled down her window. "If we listen, maybe we can hear one bugle."

"Bugle?"

They waited for ten more minutes, but the elk weren't in a talkative mood.

Into the park they traveled, and he wound around until they reached a parking lot with access to several different trails, including a fairly easy one around Bear Lake. Skye looked around as he helped her out of the truck. Could she feel the difference up here in the mountains? Were these beautiful surroundings winning her over?

"Now we hike?" She lifted her sneaker-clad foot and twisted it around, as if stretching for a race.

"Now we go explore God's creation." He reached into the bed of his truck and pulled a couple of water bottles from a cooler. They went into his backpack, joining granola bars, some trail mix, and a few first-aid items he never left behind when he hiked.

"Show me the way, oh Fearless Leader." Skye motioned around them.

He shook his head and grabbed her fingers. "You're going to love it."

She made a noncommittal noise but walked along beside him without pulling free.

As this was one of the more popular trails, they were never alone for more than a few minutes. And the loop itself was less than a mile long. They kept an easy pace the short distance to the water, and then he stopped to take in the view, just like always.

Mountains, still with just a bit of snow up top, framed the

small lake. Pines stood tall around it like guards watching over the still waters. Bugs hovered in swarms, but they found a spot with fewer and stood near the water.

"Worth coming up here?" He almost hated to break the quiet, but he had to know what went on behind those expressive eyes of hers.

"It's very pretty."

"Do you want to walk around the loop? Or go back and try a different trail?"

Her shoulders rose in a shrug. "You're the one who planned today. What do you recommend?"

"This trail wouldn't take very long. But some of the others have some waterfalls and such. This is pretty much the view for this one."

"I like waterfalls."

"Let's go, then."

Back at the trailhead, he picked one with a bit more rise to it. They'd have to work a little harder, but the vistas were beautiful and not too far off. Half an hour later, she tugged him to a stop and bent over, grasping her side.

"Give me a minute."

"Sorry." Spotting a log, he steered her in that direction so she could sit, then handed her a water bottle. "I sometimes forget you're not used to this altitude like I am."

"Altitude. Exercise. Any of it." She took a long drink before screwing the cap back on. "Whew. I thought you said these were easy trails."

"This is an easy trail." He chuckled. "It's nothing like a fourteener."

"A fourteener?"

"A hike that goes up at least fourteen thousand feet in elevation. Like Long's Peak."

"Do I dare ask how close we are to that right now?"

"Not even close." He couldn't stop another small laugh. "Around ninety-five hundred, maybe."

She took another drink and shook her head. "And people willingly go higher?"

"The views are pretty amazing. I did a fourteener with some friends last year. Nothing like the exhilaration when you reach the top."

"And I thought I liked to find thrills." She stood again, something he interpreted as respect in her eyes. "You win on that one. I don't think I could handle it."

"You might be surprised what you can do when you put your mind to it." He wove his fingers through hers once more, and they continued up the path at a slightly slower pace.

Not much later, he caught sight of something he knew would be a hit. Had she seen it yet? Did she realize what it was? It was rare for the stuff to remain this late in the summer, but this corner was pretty shaded.

Was that snow? Skye froze in her tracks but not from the temperature. She'd actually been rather warm up until now, but nothing else could explain the white covering the ground just ahead of her. Could it?

Only one way to find out. She tugged free of Benjamin's grip—not that she minded as much as she should that he'd woven their fingers together this whole time—and rushed ahead and up the hill. Crunch, crunch went the stuff under her feet. As her fingers wrapped some up, the iciness stung against her flushed skin. Snow. In early July.

"You okay there, Skye?" Benjamin's voice was laced with laughter once again.

Well, two could find a reason to laugh at this. She fisted a bit more of the cold, crusty crystals and chucked the ball at him in a sudden attack. It splattered all over his chest in such a satisfying way, she couldn't resist doing it again.

"Hey!"

But he had no time to duck before she lobbed another. This one grazed the side of his head, leaving a bright red ear behind. One of his dark brown brows lifted, and he charged up the hill after her.

She shrieked and dove for more ammunition, but before she could form more than another ball, he'd sent one her way, whacking her in the shoulder. This was old snow, harder than when it had first fallen, and the icy crust of it stung her skin. No wonder he was retaliating.

She tossed hers back at him as he moved to make another. It left a wet spot on his back, but then he caught her with another in the belly. There wasn't a ton of snow in this section, but it provided just enough fodder for them to wage war for five more minutes.

When they were down to more mud than snow, they both held up their hands in surrender, each gasping from laughter and exertion. He pointed toward a larger boulder not too far away, and she nodded before joining him. A hard seat, but better than the soggy ground.

He reached over and brushed some of her hairs off her cheek, tucking them behind her ear. "Glad you came?"

"I can honestly say I've never had a snowball fight in July before. So that was pretty epic." And her grin wouldn't go away even as she sat and caught her breath.

"I'm glad we could still find some. It's usually all gone by now except for higher up. I guess the conditions must have been just perfect right here."

"Seemed perfect to me." A giggle escaped her. "Thanks for dragging me up here."

"You're welcome." Something in his voice drew her attention, and she realized his hand still hovered where he'd moved her hair a moment before. A seriousness filled his eyes, and this close she could see darker blue ringing the lighter part near his pupils. He inched a bit closer, and her heart skipped a beat.

He was going to kiss her.

Her pulse accelerated from the anticipation, as well as fear. If she let him make this move, there was no going back. No denying that they'd crossed over into new territory. No trying to avoid him.

Is that what she wanted? She'd only been halfheartedly fighting to stay away from him as it was. Today was proof of that. Should she let him kiss her? Could she resist?

And then his lips pressed against hers, and the decision was out of her hands. Her breath stopped, caught in the lump in her throat. His fingers slipped around to the back of her head and drew her closer, all while his lips caressed hers in a way she'd never experienced before.

Her hand found its way to his shoulder and she leaned in, soaking in his strength and sureness and stability. She'd never wanted anything like that before. Had she lost her mind—herself? Had the altitude gotten to her?

He slowly pulled back, his lips lingering for one more second, then another, as if unwilling to leave hers quite yet. He pressed another kiss to her cheek and then her forehead before leaning his head against hers.

"Skye." Her name came out in a whisper.

"We shouldn't have done that." She squeezed her eyes closed.

The warmth of his skin disappeared as he sat back. "What?"

"I shouldn't have let you do that." She rubbed her fingers over her face. "I don't do this. I don't kiss guys. I have my

FLIRTS, and I go on to the next one. I'm not like this. I don't kiss someone when I know I'm not staying."

"What if you did stay?"

What if she did? The question took a more solid form in her mind where it had been only a vapor before. Was it possible?

"I don't even have a job. I don't have anything. I'm living off my sister." She stood and paced a few feet away, hoping the space would help clear her muddled brain.

"But that doesn't mean you can't find a job here. Have you even searched in this area?" He stood, too, but stayed next to the rock.

She shook her head. The idea hadn't even occurred to her. "That wasn't the plan."

He didn't respond.

A laugh closer to a sob bubbled up in her chest. "Who am I kidding? I don't plan. I'm more of a wing-it girl. The only thing I sort of plan is when I'm going on a trip. And even then, I only tend to plan the minimum and then look for fun things when I get there."

The words gushed from her faster than the waterfall he'd promised.

"I'm not actually asking you to plan anything right now." He stepped closer and caught her as she paced his way again.

"But you kissed me. And you said I was becoming a priority. And those things have meanings. Like you're wanting something more serious than I can offer. I told you when we first met that I don't do marriage and forever and settling down and—"

He captured her hands in his, stopping their wild waving. "Skye, slow down. All I wanted today was to kiss you."

Her heart tripped another beat.

"Honestly, I've wanted to for a while, but I didn't want ... well, this. I was afraid it would scare you. And I was right. But you're overreacting a bit right now. I just got wrapped up in the moment, seeing you so happy and carefree and full of life. I couldn't resist."

He pulled her to him, holding her tight against his chest. "I'm not sorry I gave in. Because it was the best kiss of my life. And, honestly, I might want a repeat in the near future."

"But nothing more serious?" The question wouldn't stay trapped inside her. She had to ask. Had to know.

"I can't promise I won't ever want more than just an amazing friendship full of fun dates and sweet kisses with you. But that doesn't mean we have to rush from one to the other right away. We can work up to it. See where this thing goes. I mean, until I convince you that you could be happy living out here, there's not much point in it, anyway, right?"

His voice was a bit wistful, but she couldn't promise him more today. Might not ever be able to though a tiny part of her wished to take the sadness away.

"Right."

"Okay, then." He leaned back and grinned at her. "Should we go find that waterfall and then head back down so we can grab a bite on the way back?"

"Sure."

He twined their fingers together once more as if nothing else had happened, and led her around the trail. The waterfall wasn't much farther. Its waters rushed down the mountain-side in gurgles and splashes and a dull roar. It rather reminded her of her insides right now, all churned up and confused and swirling around with new emotions.

"See? It's not so bad hiking, right?" He pressed a kiss to her temple but left it at that. After a few quick photos and moments of admiring God's handiwork, he led her back the way they came.

And the longer they walked, the more she found she could

get used to following his lead. Yet another new and scary notion. This day had been full of them.

Maybe that's why, as he dropped her off later that afternoon, she heard herself saying, "Do you still need a plus one for those weddings?"

"Only if it's you."

And there went her heart again, missing more beats. Could she blame it on the thinner air? Or was there more at work in all this? It was just to help him out in keeping the table numbers even, right?

15

"You about ready to be off duty?" Rain took a basket of bubbles from Skye's hands.

"I'm not sure I'll actually be 'off duty' when I stop working with you." Skye tried to play it cool as she relinquished the last of her given tasks.

"It's a wedding reception. You eat and hang out with Benjamin. How is that like work?"

Skye didn't answer. What could she say? She didn't even understand why she was nervous about this evening. Her gaze moved to the door of the auditorium, where family pictures were wrapping up.

"Something has changed between you two." Rain's comment drew Skye's attention back to her sister.

"Hmm?"

"You've been different ever since he took you hiking last Thursday." Rain narrowed her eyes.

"Have I?"

"Yes. And I wonder why."

Saved by the bridal party. They filtered out of the auditorium laughing and smiling, all headed for the reception down the hallway. Benjamin's eyes met hers, and her tummy roiled underneath her floral chiffon dress.

Even though he looked different without the normal bowtie, the wheat-colored suitcoat over the light blue shirt was a nice combination. The pink boutonniere brought out the pink in his plaid skinny tie. Her heart tripped over itself as he headed her way.

"Here's the most beautiful date in the whole building." He drew her arm through his.

"You shouldn't say that. Your sister is a gorgeous bride." Skye pushed the protest out past a lump in her throat.

"Even if it's true?" His voice was pitched low where only she could hear.

"It's not true." Halfheartedly she poked his arm. "Stop it."

"I'm not so convinced." He pressed a kiss to her cheek just as Rain looked their way.

So much for keeping that aspect of their relationship a secret from her sister. Rain said nothing, but her narrowed eyes showed disapproval. Skye would wait to worry about that later because Benjamin led her toward the fellowship hall.

Rain had done a great job of decking out the room in a way that made it seem magical. Twinkle lights draped from the edges of the ceiling to meet in the middle, creating an almost tent-like atmosphere. The round tables were draped in pristine white cloths, tea lights adding to the romantic ambiance. Their nameplates had them seated with one of Benjamin's aunts and uncles, three cousins, and his maternal grandmother.

It hadn't even crossed her mind that by agreeing to be his date tonight, she also set herself up to meet his whole family. Mentally she banged her head against a wall for a minute. Then she put on what she hoped was her most gracious smile and greeted his grandmother.

"How long have you two been an item?" Aunt Hattie asked.

"Oh, we're not—"

Benjamin's answer intercepted hers. "I met Skye earlier this summer. Her sister is Amelia's wedding planner."

He covered her hand with his, and it took all her willpower not to pull away. While it had been more of a non-answer, it also left his family believing they were a real couple. Were they? Is this what she'd agreed to by conceding to come this evening?

The food was delicious. Amelia and Clark made their way around the room, greeting the people at each table, their smiles so bright they made the other lights seem dim. When they got to Benjamin and Skye, Amelia drew her into a huge hug.

"I'm so glad you agreed to be Bennie's plus one tonight." Amelia beamed.

"Glad to help keep an even number at the tables." Skye kept her voice light, hoping to play off the seriousness that had settled over her as the date's reality dawned on her.

"Oh, please. As if I care about something like that." Amelia waved her beringed hand in the air as if to shoo away a fly.

Skye flashed a slight glare at Benjamin. Hadn't that been his reason for needing a date tonight?

But his smile never dimmed as he slid his arm around her waist. "She definitely makes me look good."

That wasn't a bit true. Benjamin looked great this evening —not that she'd ever seen him look bad. Not even in those tacky swim shorts. Good grief! What was wrong with her tonight?

"Well, you need all the help you can get. It's why I insisted on this tie." Amelia tweaked his plaid with a smirk.

"But his bowties are so cute." The protest came out before Skye could snatch it back.

"Oh, really?" Benjamin turned her way with an expression of pleasure.

"I mean, in a nerdy kind of way." Skye shrugged, but it was too late to play it off as much as she'd like.

"Well, either way, thank you for agreeing to take pity on my brother and come tonight. I'm so glad you're here this summer. Bennie's been so much happier lately."

And on that note, the bride flitted away to talk to other guests, and Skye slumped into her seat. She was in trouble. No other word for it.

"You okay?" Benjamin's whisper made her jump.

"Sure." Somehow she got the reply out.

"Oh, they're about to cut the cake!" Aunt Hattie turned her chair to see better.

Amelia and Clark giggled and laughed as he wrapped his arm around her and helped her push the knife through the icing. The requisite shoving of a bite in each other's faces followed, with a sweet moment where Clark helped his wife dab at the smeared frosting with a napkin.

As the guests settled in with their dessert several minutes later, Benjamin's dad stood and called for attention. "I'm not going to take too much of your time."

He motioned Amelia and Clark over next to him and pressed a kiss to her forehead. "This beautiful girl. My girl." He paused a moment to clear his throat. "I have been praying her whole life for the man who would marry her. And now she's married."

Several sighs and *ahhs* sounded around the room. Benjamin's mom dabbed at her eyes.

"Clark, this is my baby girl. And I am trusting you to take good care of her."

"I will, sir." Clark's voice cracked, too, as he wrapped an arm around his bride.

"Amelia, your mother and I are so proud of the woman you have become. We know you're going to do not only us proud as you start your new journey as Clark's wife, but him too." He squeezed her hand. "Let's all pray one more time over this couple."

Skye bowed her head just like everyone else, but her mind couldn't focus on the words. Instead, her head churned with jealousy and doubts. Benjamin squeezed her fingers, and she realized the prayer was over.

"What's wrong?" He leaned close so no one else would be able to hear their conversation.

Skye shook her head. "I don't know."

He glanced around and then tugged her up and through the milling crowd getting their bubbles ready. Down a hallway, away from the melee, he stopped next to a counter normally used for the church greeters. Today it was covered in various wedding paraphernalia so Rain could grab whatever she needed to ensure things ran smoothly.

"Skye, what's wrong?" Benjamin repeated his question.

She blinked, surprised to feel a tear slip from her eye.

When he pulled her into his chest, she nestled in, her cheek against his stupid tie. She'd never sought comfort from a guy before, but nothing in the world felt as right as being here at this moment. A sob broke from somewhere deep inside her, surprising her even more. Normally she wasn't a crier.

His hand rubbed circles on her back, and he swayed, as if rocking a small child. And deep inside, the small child who had longed for a daddy to love her like Amelia's obviously did crumbled another chunk of her emotional walls.

"What's it like?" Skye's question muffled against his shirt.

"Hmm?" He pulled back a few inches and lifted her face, his thumb rubbing some of the moisture from her cheek.

"What was it like?"

"What was what like?"

"Growing up with a dad like that? One who obviously loves you guys and cares what happens in your life?" Bitterness laced her voice, but she couldn't help it.

"But surely your dad loves you, too, Skye." Benjamin's forehead wrinkled in a frown.

"Can you love an obligation and a responsibility?" Skye folded her arms around her middle. "That's all I am to him."

"Skye!" Rain stood at the edge of the counter, mouth open, eyes wide.

Benjamin glanced between the two sisters, uncertainty lining his normally sure movements.

Rain blinked a few times and then turned her attention to him. "Your sister is about to leave. I was coming to find you so you could join in blowing bubbles." She thrust a couple of small tubes in his hand, shot a glare at Skye, and then spun on her heel and marched away.

"You should go catch her." Benjamin squeezed Skye's arm.

"I'm sure she'll catch me later." Skye shook her head. "But you should go join your family."

"Want to come too?" He offered her one of the bottles.

"I'd only dampen the happy moment."

He paused, pressed a kiss to her cheek, and then hurried away.

Now what? She'd ruined her date. Her sister was furious. And she rode with Rain, so there was no escaping.

***

Benjamin smiled and waved his sister and new brother-in-law off, but it was a façade. He'd much rather have stayed with Skye, back in the church hallway. That was probably the most real she'd been with him ... ever.

As Amelia and Clark pulled away in their decorated car, the cans clanging on the ground behind them, he loosened his tie, noticing it was damp from Skye's tears. Maybe she'd still be where he left her, and they could talk more about what she'd said. Because in all his conversations and interactions with Rain over the last few years, he'd never gotten the impression that she'd lacked a good family back in Missouri.

Sure, their mom was gone, but wasn't Skye running around in a red convertible and wearing nice clothes, and had just graduated from a good university? All because her dad made sure she had everything she needed and more? He undid his top button and sighed. Maybe he should stay out of it and let the sisters work things out on their own, but his feet turned him back where he'd been moments before.

No sign of Skye near the table. Rain stuffed things in plastic boxes, her movements jerky and harsh. She glanced up as he approached, her jaw set tight.

"If you're looking for Skye, I sent her to the auditorium to gather candles." She snapped the lid on the top of the tub. "I assumed your date was over, so I apologize if you needed her for something else."

"Hey." He laid a hand on top of the box before she could turn away. "I'm sorry I stole your help this evening. Though I'm not, at the same time. Because something in there affected your sister in a way I've never seen before."

A bit of the iciness melted from Rain's frame. "I haven't seen her cry since she was little. She doesn't cry."

"Maybe this is progress. Maybe she just needs to work through whatever this is before she can move on and figure out what she wants to do with her life."

"Benjamin, are you sure you know what you're doing?" Rain's brows pressed together. "Skye doesn't settle. She doesn't do long-term anything. I'm amazed she agreed to two months here."

"I think something is changing in her." He glanced over his shoulder toward the auditorium. "Maybe she just hadn't found something worth settling for before now."

Rain shook her head. "I'm very afraid you're about to end up with a broken heart. Part of me wishes I'd never suggested you two go to dinner that first time."

"I'm not sorry." He rapped his knuckles against the counter. "Don't give up on her yet."

Only a few steps away, Rain's words stopped him again.

"She's wrong, you know. Dad doesn't think of us as obligations and responsibilities. He does love us. He just shows it in different ways than your dad."

Glancing over her shoulder, he gave a short nod. "Well, maybe we need to help her see that."

"I don't think she's going to listen to me."

"Then say it a different way. Maybe you're not speaking her language."

His legs ate up the length of the hallway, and then he stepped into the auditorium, mostly bare of decorations already. Rain must have worked in here during the reception. Movement on the stage drew his attention.

Skye blew out a candle and then carefully removed it from the holder, giving it a few moments to let the wax dry before laying it in the tub beside her. Only a few remained, and with half the overhead lights out, it left her in a dimness that matched the mood emanating from her.

"Know what I wish?" He walked up the aisle, pacing himself about as slowly as the bridesmaids had earlier.

She turned, a still-lit candle in hand.

"I wish I could have had you by my side the whole evening instead of just part of it." He stepped onto the stage.

"And what would I have done up here while you played the groomsman?" Skye lifted a brow.

Leaning forward, he blew out the flame between them and then pressed a kiss to her lips. "You could've stood with your arm linked through mine and watched the ceremony from the proximity I got to see it."

She rolled her eyes. "No, thank you. I got to be that close at Rain's wedding. I'm good."

"Still against weddings, then?" He caught her before she could turn away.

"I'm still the same person I was at the beginning of the summer." Her body was stiff as he pulled her back against him. "Just working this job to try and save my car."

"Hmm." He wrapped his arms over hers and nestled his cheek to hers. "That's a shame."

"A shame I'm still the same person?" She tugged as if to get away.

"No. A shame you don't like weddings." He refused to relinquish his hold on her. She felt too good snuggled in close. "I was going to ask you to be my date to Chet's wedding in a couple of weeks."

"I'm not sure it's a good idea. Look how badly it worked out today."

"Did it work out badly?" Easing her around to where she faced him, he ran a finger down her cheek. "I mean, I got to sit next to you through the meal and cake. And you complimented the way I looked ... as well as my normal bowties."

The corner of her lips turned up. "You're crazy."

"Maybe so, but you can't deny it works for me."

She snorted and then buried her face in his shoulder. "What are we doing, Benjamin?"

"Right now?" He glanced down. "Hugging. Talking."

Her head rolled back and forth. "You know that's not what

I mean. This can't go anywhere. I'm leaving in just over a month. What are we doing?"

"I believe the term is dating."

"To what end?"

"Who said there has to be an end?"

When she raised her head, he could see the battle about to come his way before she even opened her mouth. "Benj."

She'd shortened his name? The pleasure of it kept him from hearing the first few words that came after.

"—got to stop. This is only going to make it harder for both of us at the end of the summer. Maybe we shouldn't—"

Before she could continue down that road of thought, he covered her mouth with his hand. "Or maybe we should start researching job opportunities in this area and see if we can find a way for you to stay."

Tugging from his arms, she went to the next candle without saying anything.

"What's holding you back from considering that possibility?" He snuffed the flame on the taper farthest from her.

"I don't know." She laid a couple of candles in the box.

"Pray about it." He laid his beside hers and then grabbed her hands and squeezed them. "Please."

Her lips pinched together, but after a few seconds, she nodded.

He'd take it. What other choice did he have? He'd already pushed her quite a bit tonight. If he pushed too much, it would only encourage her to run away.

16

The back *yard* of his townhouse was nothing to boast about. It wasn't the reason he'd bought the property in the first place. But tonight, he had grand plans for it.

With a hope and a prayer, he plugged in the lights he'd strung across the patio area. They lit up, and he let loose the breath he'd been holding. Mark *mood lighting* off the list. The screen was in place against one of the fences. New chairs with deep cushions lined the other, with a metal firepit full of sticks in the middle.

Would Skye approve?

Sure, it was simply roasting hot dogs and marshmallows over a fire and watching a television show together, but would being outside make it exciting enough? He glanced around one more time. What was he forgetting?

Ding dong.

Too late now. She was here. His heart raced as he quickly walked through the living area to open the door.

"Hi." Skye wore her hair in two braids this evening, which

looked perfect with her light pink shorts overalls. How was it possible she made every single outfit look amazing?

"Benjamin?" She waved a hand in front of his face, and he realized he'd been gawking.

"Sorry." He stepped back. "Come on in."

"You look a little frazzled. Am I early?"

"Nope. Right on time." He grabbed her fingers and led her through the kitchen and out the back door. "What do you think?"

Skye spun in a circle, taking in the whole setup. "This is so cute!"

Another relieved breath exited his lungs. Why was it so important to make this girl happy? How had she become one of the biggest priorities in his life in only a few weeks?

"Are we watching a movie?" Her question pulled him from his thoughts.

"I thought it would be fun to introduce you to *Mork and Mindy*. You know, since you've seen the house now. So I downloaded several episodes and thought we could watch them out here later, when it's darker."

That was the only problem with trying to have an outdoor show during the summer. Longer daylight hours. But he hadn't had any better ideas, so he'd stuck with this one.

"Huh." So much for her staying impressed.

"And, until then, I can build us a fire, and we can roast hot dogs and marshmallows to our hearts' content."

"Roasted marshmallows are the best."

"Agreed." He knelt next to the firepit. "I think everything is laid out on the counter in the kitchen if you want to grab some things while I start this."

"Sure."

Using the trick his dad had taught him years before, he stuffed some dryer lint down among the sticks and branches and then nestled some newspaper around that. The dryer lint never failed to be the best fire starter ever, and a blaze quickly danced to life and licked up the pieces of wood.

"That looks good." Skye stepped back through the door, arms laden with plates and hot dogs. "Do you have some roasting forks?"

"Yes. They're here." He opened a cabinet next to the back door and dug around until he found a couple. He'd asked for them the same Christmas he'd requested the fire pit but hadn't had much chance to use either before now since he hardly ever had anyone over.

"Great." She accepted one and slid a wiener onto the end. "I'm starving."

"How come it seems you're always hungry or needing to eat when we're together?" He slid his own dog onto a fork and sat in the chair beside hers.

"Really?" She cast him a glance from the corner of her eye. "You're the one who set this up at seven. I'm used to eating earlier."

"Fair enough. I just wanted to make sure we didn't do it too early since the sun won't go down for a while yet."

"Rain asked what we were doing, and I told her I had no idea." Skye flipped her hot dog over to roast the other side. "I don't think I could've guessed this even if I'd tried. But it's so fun. I like these chairs."

"Thanks."

"They're nice and big, huh? Almost big enough two could sit in them side by side."

Now, there was a thought. Maybe they could snuggle while watching the show instead of just sitting beside each other. Much nicer.

When he looked over her way, he caught a grin that said

maybe she thought along the same lines. At least he hoped that's what it meant.

"You're burning." She pointed to the end of his fork, where his meat blackened. He didn't even care, but he rotated it anyway.

They settled in a few minutes later, each with their hot dog loaded the way they liked it, chips and fruit piled on their plates. Skye let out a contented sigh as she took a big bite. And he couldn't stop the bubble of pleasure that welled up inside of him at the sound.

"How's your job search going?" The question escaped from his lips before he could think better of it.

And there went all signs of contentment from her beautiful face.

"About as well as it has the whole summer." Her nose wrinkled. "If I wanted to be an office manager or an assistant or something like that, there are tons of opportunities. But nothing that actually interests me."

"Even around here?"

She rolled her eyes. "Yes. Because I have time to search for jobs across the whole country, Benjamin. While folding wedding programs and tying up bird seed pouches."

He swallowed the hurt at knowing she still hadn't expanded her search to near him. "It's just one area, not a whole country."

"Right. Sorry, counselor."

So they were back to that again. Was she rebuilding her walls after he'd begun to knock them down? Not if he could help it.

"I'm not arguing with you. Just pointing out there are opportunities in other places than St. Louis. Possibly something even better since this is a college town." He rose before she could offer a comeback. "Ready for marshmallows?"

She followed him into the kitchen instead of staying on the patio. "Are you changing the subject?"

"I thought you didn't want to talk about the other one." He tugged the bag until a hole opened big enough to grab one of the jumbo marshmallows. "Can you grab the chocolate and graham crackers?"

She squeaked her protest but did as he asked. Back outside, he stirred up the embers and added a couple of thick sticks to keep the flames going longer. She flopped down and tossed the chocolate at him.

"Thanks."

She huffed and crossed her arms over her chest.

"Why are you mad now? I was only trying to follow your lead."

"You didn't let me finish. You just pointed out your ideas and then jumped to dessert."

"You like dessert." He poked a fork through a couple of marshmallows and handed it to her.

"I do. But you're doing it again."

"Tell me. What were you going to say?" He turned to face her more fully.

"I just don't want to have to talk about job searching with you when it's all I get from Rain and my father. He never texts except to ask if I've found something yet or to remind me that my car is on the line." Skye's hands flopped in her lap, the roasting fork clattering to the pavement. "I just wanted one evening where I didn't have to think about it. Didn't have it hanging over my head."

He moved over, and just like she'd hinted at earlier, they both fit in the wide chair, though just barely.

"Come here." His arm pulled her to him, and he pressed a kiss to her forehead. "I'm sorry. I wanted to help, but I obviously went about it the wrong way. I don't want to see you unhappy, and I know how much you love that car."

A giggle escaped. "I'm sorry. The further into the summer we get, the more frustrating it is to find nothing. To know my father will win, and I will be trapped with no car and no way to get out from under him."

"Is he really that bad?"

She pulled back and stared up at the sky in time to see the first star twinkle to life. "It's complicated. You know my mom died when I was young. Thirteen. Rain sort of took over as a mother figure, but she's only four years older. And our father buried himself in work. It became more important to him than anything else—including us."

"Why doesn't Rain feel the same way about your dad?"

Skye shrugged. "I have no idea. Maybe because she was basically old enough to leave when it all happened. She wasn't around to see him retreat into his company, into making more money, expanding his empire. And then she got married right out of college."

Shifting to a more comfortable position, she leaned into his strength.

He let out a slow breath. "We'll just have to find you something soon so he can't take that silly little car away."

"It's not silly." She lightly shoved him. "And I have no idea what kind of job you think you could find."

"Maybe we'll just have to expand your search a bit." He leaned over and grabbed the marshmallow bag. "But we have other things to do this evening."

"I definitely like the idea of other things besides a job search." She gratefully accepted the pillowy treats and reloaded her roasting fork.

"S'mores and classic TV. Can't beat that."

A smile spread her lips. Who was this guy? All serious and firm one minute, then soft and silly the next. And why was she so drawn to him when no other guy had captivated her before?

Whatever the reason, she decided to figure it out later. Because sitting under the darkening sky, his lights twinkling above, an old sitcom flashing on the screen across from them, and his arm around her, how could she think of anything else? If she weren't officially a Missouri resident, she might be in danger of falling in love. Good thing everything about this summer was temporary.

Three episodes later, she pulled herself away and drove back to Rain's house—after he bestowed one of the sweetest goodnight kisses she'd ever had. They both had a busy schedule the next day, and she feared if she stayed much longer, she'd be completely under his spell. Not an option at this point in her life.

Maybe all the weddings she'd been helping with were getting to her—scrambling her brain. Because she began to think forever with Benjamin Smith might not be so bad. And she couldn't let her mind or heart go down that road.

"You're back." Rain straightened from where she dug through the fridge.

"I'm back. You weren't waiting up for me, were you?"

"No. I'm just munchy and came down to see if anything sounded good."

"In that fridge? No way. The only foods that sound good after ten at night are junk food, and you don't keep enough of that around here." Skye held up a finger. "Hang on a minute."

She dashed down the stairs and grabbed a bag of chocolate-covered pretzels from her nightstand. Back up and to where her sister waited, one brow raised.

"You're welcome." Skye turned to go back down but

stopped when her sister cleared her throat. They hadn't spoken much in the five days since Amelia's wedding, so Skye hadn't expected a conversation now.

"Did you have fun?" Rain leaned against the counter and bit into one of the snacks.

"I did."

"What did you guys do tonight?"

"Benjamin set up an outdoor theater on his patio. We roasted hotdogs and s'mores over the firepit and watched old episodes of this really weird TV show he likes."

Rain shook her head.

"What?"

"Jeremiah and I sat and watched television tonight too, but you'd say we were boring."

"Did you watch it under the stars?" Skye folded her arms around her middle.

"Nope. We have a nice comfy couch that isn't anywhere near the mosquitoes." Rain crunched another pretzel.

"To each her own, I guess. The chairs on Benjamin's patio were comfy."

"Don't you ever get tired of it?"

Skye's back straightened. "Of what?"

"Of needing something new and different every time you go out. Of always looking for an adventure or a place you haven't tried yet." Rain motioned around her living area. "Don't you ever want to just be boring one night?"

"Why would I want to be boring?"

"Because sometimes, doing something you always do is more relaxing. You don't have to think about it or try to make it exciting. It's comfortable."

Skye shook her head. "Maybe that's your style, but it's not mine."

"One day, you're going to wake up and realize you're

exhausted. And that no one is going to want to have to deal with having to keep you entertained and adventured. When that happens, you might end up alone. Will your adventures be as much fun then?"

Skye pinched her lips together, swallowing against the tears burning her eyes. Her sister attacked her almost as much as their father did lately. And it was hours since Benjamin's arms held her tight and gave her hope that all would work out by summer's end.

"Benjamin doesn't seem to mind that I don't always want to do the same things. He set tonight up all by himself."

"But for how long, Skye? How long can he keep it up? Eventually, he might repeat himself. Would you be okay with that?"

"I'm not a snob, Rain. I don't mind going to a restaurant more than once. Especially if it's good." She grabbed back her now half-empty bag of pretzels. "Besides, he knows I'm leaving in a few weeks. He's just trying to make the rest of my stay fun."

"You sure he knows that?" Rain's question haunted her as she headed back down to the basement.

Didn't he? Did she still know that? What was going on with her tonight?

She tossed her snacks back on the nightstand and changed into pj's. She still had to get through the two weddings Rain had scheduled this weekend—though at least she didn't have to wrangle any flower girls. Then Benjamin's cousin's wedding was next weekend. Two weeks after that, Rain would slow down enough not to need Skye as much anymore.

What then?

That was the convertible-worthy question, wasn't it?

Flopping back on the bed, she covered her eyes with her arm. *What do you want me to do, God? And what do I do about Benjamin?*

17

Later the next week, Skye blinked her eyes a few times as she tried to focus on arranging a stack of wedding programs in a neat and pretty manner. Could programs look pretty? If they could, wedding programs would be the ones to do it.

Exhaustion weighed down her limbs. When was the last time she'd slept through the night without the dreams? They varied each night but contained similar elements—a convertible driving away, a job chaining her to a desk, a wedding dress trying to choke her. Combined, they ruined any hope of returning to a restful sleep.

A *ding* from her phone startled her.

> Do you still have your bridesmaid dress? BC
> Guess what!

Bree Henley had been Skye's friend for four years. She and Katie Wilhite were Skye's road-trip buddies during college. When their last girls' trip together earlier that summer backfired by ending Bree's engagement a month before her wedding, Skye had worked behind the scenes with Bree's former fiancé's brother and Katie to secretly send them on their honeymoon together.

A cruise sounded really nice right about now. But Bree's cruise had been canceled by a hurricane, and she and Nathan had ended up spending several days together in Dallas, Texas. Not nearly as romantic, but maybe it worked anyway?

> Of course, I still have my bridesmaid dress.

> Good, because the wedding is back on! We're setting it for October this time. To coincide with fall break. I got a new job too!

Apparently, Bree had all the luck this summer. Skye shook herself and rolled her eyes. What was she thinking? It wasn't like she wanted a romance of her own—not that she hadn't accidentally stumbled on something that was more and more undeniably like a romance as the weeks went on. And there was no way she wanted to teach—the only position Bree could've found that would let her have a fall break.

> Congrats! Send me details, and I'll do my best to be there!

> Did you find a job yet? How's Colorado?

> Colorado is ...

Skye's thumbs hovered over the keypad. What to say?

Her mind ran through images of the mountains, the water-fall and snow, the flowers, the people. Colorado had been a trip like none of her others. In good ways and bad.

Colorado is gorgeous. But no job yet.

That would have to do for now. Maybe she could catch up with Bree soon. After she got her head back on straight and had real news instead of just confusion.

Praying for a job to come your way soon!
Miss you!

Miss you too.

And she did miss Bree and Katie. They'd be much more understanding than Rain had been this summer. Or at least try to be.

She folded a few more of the seemingly never-ending pile of wedding programs. How many people did this bride invite to her wedding? A glance at the names, and Skye realized these were for Benjamin's cousin Chet. In other words, she was supposed to be at this wedding too.

How could she get out of this one? Or anything else he might want to do together for the next few weeks? That's all she had left before she would head back to Missouri and turn in her car keys. Assuming she didn't find a job. And the odds of that looked slimmer with every online search, even after expanding to this area.

Another chime of her phone. What had Bree forgotten?

No, not Bree. Her father.

Talked to my associate Harvey Sims. He's got a spot open and said to send you in for an interview as soon as you get home.

No greeting. No query as to whether or not she'd found something on her own. Simply an assumption that she'd be there and still need his help to find a position. But Harvey Sims? The accountant? Numbers were okay, but the marketing degree her father had insisted on could be used in so many better ways than as an assistant in a tax firm.

I'll keep that in mind.

He wouldn't like that response, but he didn't like when his texts went completely unanswered either. And it was the best she could do. She couldn't offer thanks for something she didn't want or make promises she had no intention of keeping.

You'll do better than that. You'll go talk to him unless you have something else lined up already. Or have you decided to give the car back?

Her car. Skye sighed and glanced out the window where her red beauty sat waiting for her. If the car wasn't part of this agreement, she'd throw caution the rest of the way to the wind and hitchhike around the country for a while. Or empty her savings and go backpack around Europe. Why not live while she was young enough to enjoy it?

She pressed down on the middle of a program before realizing she had it crooked. Scowling, she tossed it aside. Rain could decide if they could do without one of these multiple hundreds of itineraries. If all else failed, it could be hers. And there she went again, considering herself as Benjamin's plus one to be a given.

Are you ignoring me?

Oops. She hadn't replied to that last text from her father. She picked up the phone and debated what to say.

> I'm not ignoring you. I was working on a project for Rain.

> Well, I'm glad to know you're working while you're there and not just playing around.

Skye let out a feral growl, banging her hands against the counter.

Rain poked her head around the corner. "Everything okay in here?"

"Just dandy." Skye spit the words out between gritted teeth.

"Want to talk about it?" Rain walked over and picked up the misshapen program but didn't say anything about its warped crease.

"Not really."

"I'm a good listener."

"You wouldn't understand." Skye mashed another program into submission and set it on the pile.

"Try me." Rain crossed her arms.

"Our father has asked Harvey Sims to give me an interview for a position at his firm when I get home."

"There ya go. You said you couldn't find any jobs. Problem solved."

"Problem *not* solved." Skye ignored the *ding* of her phone. Probably their father wanting to know why she hadn't replied again. "I didn't say I couldn't find any jobs. I said I couldn't find anything that sounded like something I want to do for the rest of my life."

Rain propped a hip against the corner of the counter. "What is it about Harvey Sims's position that you don't want?"

"Well, for one, I never wanted to be an accountant. Stuck behind a desk forever. Crunching other people's numbers.

Sounds tedious and boring." Skye held up a finger. "For two, you know Harvey Sims."

"Okay, I'll give you the second point." Rain's lips twisted to the side. "Mr. Sims is a bit … much."

"Thank you."

The chime of her phone reminded her she hadn't acknowledged the first one.

"Need to get that?" Rain pointed to the device.

"It's our father. Probably furious because I didn't type out a response to his last tirade. I thought it better to cool off before sending a reply."

Rain grabbed the phone before Skye could stop her. She stepped far enough away from the counter that Skye couldn't reach without having to go around, and by that time Rain had skimmed through the conversation. She handed the device back but didn't look a bit remorseful.

"He thinks you're ignoring him."

Skye pulled up the latest text.

> No response makes me think maybe you are playing more than working.

She closed her eyes and inhaled slowly, letting the air flare her nostrils and fill her lungs to capacity before slowly allowing it to leak back out into the atmosphere. Her heartrate remained too high, but at least it wasn't lightspeed anymore. Lips pursed, she typed out a reply that probably wouldn't be appreciated but was the best she could do.

> Still working. The office closes at six. I'll have more time to talk then.

Hopefully he wouldn't take that as an offer to call her later this evening.

"Tell me more about this perfect job you're looking for." Rain wasn't helping Skye calm down any.

"I don't know."

"You don't know what you're looking for?"

"Right."

"No wonder you haven't found anything yet."

Skye returned to her spot behind the counter. It was safer to have at least a small barrier between her and her sister right now. She creased another program, but Rain snatched the rest of the stack away from her.

"You're going to ruin more than you help in this mood." She set them aside along with the wonky one from earlier. "Help me understand. What have you tried searching for?"

"I have been doing every kind of search I can think of. But mostly, I get office jobs or really weird things like truck driving or warehouse security. Nothing I want to do."

"As much as you like to drive and see different places, I would think driving a truck would be right up your alley."

"Ha." Skye shook her head. "No way. Driving my car is one thing. But a big rig? No, thank you. And it's not like they get to decide where they're going."

"So, you want something not in an office but not in a truck?" Rain leaned her elbows on the counter.

"I want something that doesn't keep me only doing paperwork, chained to a desk all the time." Skye spread her hands out in front of her. "Maybe even that allows for a bit of travel. Something that can be fun. That I can look forward to doing every day."

"You do realize that pretty much any job you find will come with at least some paperwork, right?" Rain hooked a thumb over her shoulder. "I mean, I have to file forms and make sure everything is on the up and up with taxes and the various merchants I work with. But it's worth it to have to do the boring part because the rest of it is fun. Well, except for the beastly flower girls."

"Let's not talk about flower girls anytime soon, 'kay?" Skye shuddered.

"Got it." Rain smirked. "But seriously, dealing with … those … as well as the occasional bridezilla. And filing a few papers each day. Those don't seem as boring or bad when I get to help so many women enjoy the day of their dreams. To see them begin their happily ever after, that fulfils me like nothing else I've ever done."

"And I'm glad you have that, but I haven't found mine yet. Maybe there's nothing out there that can make the paperwork worth it."

"Don't give up yet." Rain tapped the back of Skye's phone that rested on the counter. "On finding a job or on making things right with Dad."

As if on cue, the device let out another *ding*. Skye sighed and turned it over. Not their father. Benjamin.

"Oh. I'm supposed to be meeting with him in half an hour!" Rain dashed into her office and came back out with her purse.

"Why?"

"Jeremiah and I are trying to be responsible and make our wills and stuff."

Skye shook her head as her sister dashed out the door. She was way too grown up for Skye sometimes. Weren't wills for when you were near death?

Her gaze moved to the text.

Just heard there's a concert at Red Rock Amphitheater next week. You interested?

The photo included was of one of her favorite bands. A

quick internet search showed her a gorgeous outdoor area where the concert would take place. Wow.

But she'd promised herself she wouldn't accept any more invitations from Benjamin—at least not after the wedding thing she was still trying to get out of.

Yet the location and music group had her yearning to say, 'Yes.'

"Just once more." She whispered as she typed out her reply.

"Okay. We've got everything set up the way you want for where your possessions and business assets will go should either or both of you pass away. I think the only thing we have left is guardianship of your future children." Benjamin tapped the end of his marker against the flowchart he'd made as he talked with Rain and Jeremiah. "Have you thought about who you might want to name as guardians?"

Rain exchanged a glance with Jeremiah. "There's obviously our parents as an option, or Jeremiah's older brother, although they already have three of their own children, so it might not be fair to him to expect him to take on more."

"Okay. So maybe Jeremiah's parents?"

Jeremiah leaned forward and tapped the tips of his fingers together. "My only concern is that my parents are already in their sixties. Assuming we have a child in the next year, they'll be getting up there by the time the child graduates from college."

"And your dad, Rain?" Benjamin almost hesitated to ask, knowing enough of Skye's struggles with the man, but Rain didn't seem to have the same issues, and they were running out of options.

"I think he's who we'll have to go with for now." Rain

sighed heavily enough to flutter the bangs that swept over the side of her face. "I can't in good conscience name my sister."

Benjamin's breath caught. While part of him agreed with Rain's assessment of Skye's ability to take care of any nieces and nephews she might have down the road, something in his gut rebelled. If push came to shove, he knew Skye would bend over backward for any children her sister might have.

But he couldn't say all that in an official capacity as Rain's lawyer. "Your dad's full legal name?"

"Winston Laramie Jones III." Rain handed over a business card with her father's information printed on it. "We're the first generation to break the mold in a hundred years."

"That's some name." Benjamin made sure he had it written down correctly even though Rain motioned he could keep the card. If one of the legal assistants ended up putting this document together, she might not look deep enough in the file to find the small piece of cardstock. "Have you told him what you're considering?"

"We haven't. I figured there was no reason to mention it until we got pregnant, at the very earliest. It's a moot point until then."

"True. Still, make sure he knows down the road. Just in case. That way it won't be a complete shock if it comes to pass. Though I hope you never have to use that part of this document."

"We really appreciate all your help, Benjamin. I know we don't have a lot of estate value, but this at least gives us some peace of mind. And taking care of it now, before the craziness that comes with having children, is much easier than waiting until we might not be able to find as much time."

"Not a problem at all. This is my job." He shook Jeremiah's hand and then Rain's. "I have you down to come back in next week for the signing. If you think of anything else or have questions in the meantime, just let me know."

"It's not like we won't be seeing each other this weekend. You're one of Chet's groomsmen, right?"

"Yes. And I plan to steal Skye away as my plus one at the reception, too, if that works for you."

Rain's lips pinched. Right. The last time he'd done that, Rain had overheard her sister crying over their dad. Was she afraid something similar would happen this time? Or had something else put that expression on her face?

"Are you needing her to help more with this wedding? I know Chet's fiancée got a little crazy with the invite list. Not to mention the size of the wedding party. Aren't there a full dozen of us?"

"There are. It's not that." Rain ducked her head. "Never mind. Of course, she can accompany you."

"We've been friends for what? Four years now?" Benjamin folded his arms across his chest. "Want to try being honest with me?"

Jeremiah squeezed Rain's arm.

She raised her head and looked him straight in the eye. "I just wonder which of you is going to end up hurt more at the end of this summer."

"I'm not sure I know what you mean by that."

"This thing between you two. I've warned you both, but you seem determined to continue your path straight toward the edge of a cliff. There's no way she's staying here at the end of the summer. She can't even decide on a job she wants. She's flighty and irresponsible and needs to grow up. And I think she's going to break your heart."

Benjamin sat back in his seat. Well, he'd asked for it. But he had no idea Skye's own sister felt so strongly about her.

"I think you're wrong about at least some of that." His words came out quietly but loud enough to hear in his small office. "She may need to do some more growing up so she can find a job, but she's not flighty or irresponsible. Haven't you trusted her all summer with your business?"

The corner of Rain's bottom lip disappeared behind her teeth. "Ye-es."

"And has she disappointed you in anything big to do with your company?"

"No."

"She just needs to find her perfect position. But first, she needs to figure out she needs to ask for help in finding it." Benjamin straightened the papers in front of him and paper-clipped them together. "I'm still hoping she'll figure it out soon enough so that I can be the one she asks."

Rain shook her head. "You're in deeper than I thought you were, aren't you?"

"I'm in deeper than I meant to be at the beginning of the summer. But I can't deny how much I'm enjoying it." He shrugged a shoulder. "Maybe instead of always being so down on your sister, you should try listening to her side of things."

Rain's lips pinched together again. Jeremiah motioned as if to say, 'Cut and run while you can, man.'

"I have been listening to her. All summer." Rain pulled her purse strap over her shoulder. "If she really wanted to find a job, she'd find one. Instead, she's using every excuse she can think of to turn positions down."

"If you had to work as a doctor instead of a wedding planner, would you like it?" Benjamin leaned forward. "Would you find as much enjoyment and satisfaction from working in construction? Or being a receptionist?"

"That's different."

"Is it?"

When they left a few minutes later, he wondered if he'd pushed too far. Sure, he'd been friends with them much longer than he'd known Skye. But something deep inside made him want to defend her and fight for her. Would she want him to?

That was a question for another day. And he had at least two more dates scheduled with her—the wedding and the concert. Surely he could break through a bit more of her wall in that amount of time.

Jeremiah poked his head back around the door, startling Benjamin from his thoughts. "Sorry. I just wanted to let you know Rain means well."

Benjamin blinked. "Um, okay."

"I know she comes across a bit coldhearted regarding her sister. But I don't think she really knows what to do with her now." Jeremiah took another step into the office. "When their mom died, Rain had to grow up fast. She became something between a mother figure and a sister for Skye. Then, a year later, she was off to college and missed a lot of Skye's growing up."

He ran a hand through his hair and huffed. "The Skye who is spending the summer with us doesn't exactly fit the image Rain has in her head of that young teenager she used to know. It's not that she doesn't love her. It's just ... different. I don't know."

"Thanks for trying to explain things." Benjamin tapped his pencil against the desk. "I knew a little of that from Skye, but it's a different perspective for each sister. I just hope they can actually sit down and talk before the end of the summer."

"You and me both, man." Jeremiah saluted. "See you at Chet's wedding."

"I'll be the one in the bow tie."

Jeremiah chuckled as he left once again. Benjamin had forgotten that Jeremiah and Chet were buddies, and therefore Jeremiah had been roped into groomsman duty too. Maybe that would make things easier for him to have Skye as a plus one for the reception. One problem solved, anyway.

18

Three o'clock the next Thursday. Just a few more hours until Benjamin could leave and pick up Skye. Then on to Denver and the concert. He clung to the hope that she would be more like herself tonight.

At the wedding on Saturday, she'd been more closed off than he'd ever seen. Had it been because of the obvious rift between her and Rain? Or was it something to do with him?

Please, Lord, let it be a sister thing and not her getting ready to leave me behind for good.

The prayer was ridiculous. He'd gone into this knowing she planned to leave. But somewhere along the summer, he'd quit believing it.

The buzz of his phone as it danced on the surface of his desk pulled him away from thoughts too sober for a night he was supposed to have a date. Brody Anderson. A good friend from church.

"Hey, Brody. What's going on?"

"Benjamin, you do powers of attorney, right?"

"Sure." Red flags waved behind Benjamin's eyes. "What's the situation?"

"My grandfather is to the point my mom can't take care of him anymore. We've had him on a waitlist for the local nursing home for months now, and a spot just came open. But they're wanting his power of attorney stuff in order before they let him in. Said Mom can't sign everything for him without it."

"Right. When would they need it by?" His gaze darted to the clock in the corner of his computer monitor. Three-fifteen. *Please say tomorrow.*

"These spots don't stay open long at all. There are several others on the list after Grandpa. If we don't get all the paperwork turned in ASAP, they'll move on to the next person." A bit of desperation tinged Brody's voice. "I know it's late notice, but is there any way you can help us out? My mom is exhausted and needs this to happen."

"I don't have any clients the rest of the afternoon. How soon can you get your grandfather here? I'll make sure you're taken care of."

"He's at a doctor's appointment right now, and then Mom can bring him straight there. Maybe around four-thirty."

They would have to majorly push things to get this all done before five. But he couldn't leave his friend in the lurch. Having gone through something similar with his own grandmother, he knew how hard it had been on his mom. No need for Brody's mother to have to shoulder that weight any longer than necessary.

"Okay. That will allow me time to have the document ready to sign when they arrive. But I'll need his information over the phone so I can prepare everything."

"What all do you need?"

Benjamin listed off the normal things—formal spellings of the names, who all would be named as power of attorney, birthdates, and more. He also covered things like a living will and the difference between general and medical powers of attorney. Brody agreed they probably needed it all.

"I'm on it. Will you be here too? Or just your mom and Grandpa?"

"If you need me there, I can come."

Benjamin shook his head even though his friend couldn't see through the device. "No need. We'll get it taken care of. And if she needs help moving some of his things to the home this weekend, let me know. I don't think I have any plans."

"You're a lifesaver, man. Thanks so much." Brody's voice sounded much lighter.

That's why Benjamin hadn't said, 'No.' His work might not be as vital as that of a doctor, but it gave people peace. And that was important.

Now, time to get busy.

The paperwork was fairly straightforward. Inserting names and dates where needed and printing it on the right paper. Nothing nearly as complicated as the trust he'd put together for a family earlier that week.

A little after four, everything was ready and waiting. He tried to concentrate on finishing up some other small tasks. Answered a few emails. Returned a call. And still had fifteen minutes left before he expected them.

Should he text Skye to give her a head's up that he might not get away as quickly as he'd planned?

No.

Even if they got here at four-forty-five, it wouldn't take long to sign and be done and on their way with copies for the nursing home. Why worry Skye if it wasn't a certainty? He strolled out to the reception desk to make sure Fern knew he had a last-minute client coming in, but no one was there.

Maybe she stepped out to deliver mail or run to the restroom for a minute.

Both conference rooms were full—other attorneys using them for their own clients. But that was fine. If all else failed, he could use his office space.

Speaking of which ... he hurried back and made sure his desk was neat enough for others to see. Files looked much better in a standing organizer instead of all over his blotter. Blue pens were all in their cup—black ink made it too hard to tell the difference between a copy and the original.

Four-thirty came and went.

He answered a few more emails. Four-thirty-five. A stroll to the reception area showed everything empty still. He let out a slow breath.

Okay, God, what's my lesson here? Did I ruin the rest of this day?

No new messages from Brody with an update. And he didn't have Brody's mom's number, so he couldn't call her. He tried not to pace, but even sitting, a finger or foot was always moving with energy that wouldn't stay contained.

Four-forty-five. *Please, God, let them walk in now.*

Nothing.

The bell over the front door chimed at four-fifty. Benjamin's heart raced as he welcomed Brody's mom, Kathleen, and her father, Harrison. Back in his office, Benjamin showed them what he'd put together and then dashed out to find someone to witness.

One conference room was still full—that meeting running late. The other was empty, but no sign of where all those people had gone. He just needed two people. Where was Fern this afternoon? Had she been dragged into that other meeting?

Come on, God! I need a little help here.

Fern appeared just as he was about to give up. She agreed

to be one witness. But he still needed one more. Would he have to step into the hall and ask a total stranger?

Five minutes after five, he found Mr. Marston. After a quick explanation about what was going on, Marston followed him back to his office, only to discover it empty. Benjamin spun around in confusion. Where had they gone?

Another search of the entire office showed no sign of them. Just as he was getting ready to call Brody and see if he knew anything, they walked back in. Kathleen supported Harrison on one side while he shuffled along with his cane.

"So sorry. He needed a bathroom break, and I wasn't sure where you were to let you know." She looked as harried as he felt.

"Not a problem. I've rounded up our witnesses, so we should be able to wrap this up quickly."

"Great."

"Why don't you settle him here in this conference room since it's closer? I'll grab the papers, and we'll get you squared away."

Signings normally didn't take long, but Harrison had Parkinson's, which made his hands shaky and hard to use. It was painful to watch him try to keep the pen clasped the correct way as his fingers refused to cooperate. The ink appeared slowly, in jagged lines, barely legible.

"Let me run and make copies, and you'll be free to go. I know you have a million other things to handle this evening."

Fern jumped up and followed him to the copier. "Bad news. I wasn't at my desk earlier because I was dealing with this mess."

At least three lights flashed on the machine, indicating jams and other bad things. If Benjamin were a cursing man, he'd sound like a sailor right about now. The kick-the-printer-to-make-it-work-again method came to mind, but he figured the way his luck was going this afternoon, it would only make matters worse.

Ten minutes later, they had the jam cleared enough to make the copies. He pressed them into Kathleen's hands and used every ounce of willpower not to shove them out the door.

"What about payment?" Kathleen stopped right before the hallway. So close.

"We're church family. I'll find you to discuss it later. You have more important things to worry about tonight."

"Thanks so much, Benjamin."

Finally. A glance at the clock had him groaning. Five-forty-five. Skye would be going crazy.

Who was he kidding? He was already there.

Dashing into his office, he shut things down, grabbed his change of clothes, and hightailed it out the door. If they ate at the venue, they still had time to make it.

So much for attorneys being trustworthy. He was an hour late! An hour!

Skye flipped the sign on the door of Happily Ever After to CLOSED and threw the deadbolt. Maybe she'd just go back to Rain's house and call it a night. The concert held less appeal after being on pins and needles, waiting forty-five minutes.

"He's still not here?" Rain came down the stairs with a box full of tulle.

"If he is, he's playing the Invisible Man." Skye grabbed her bag and rummaged for her keys. Then remembered she'd ridden with Rain that morning because she was supposed to leave with Benjamin.

"That's unlike him. Have you tried calling?"

"No."

"Because ...?"

"Because I shouldn't have to call. He should be here when he said he would."

Rain set the box down and planted her hands on her hips. "Right. I forgot you live in a world where all is black and white."

"Whatever." Skye pulled out her phone, but there were no missed calls from him. "Do you plan to stay here much longer this evening? Or can I catch a ride with you?"

"A ride where? I thought you had plans."

"We did have plans. But evidently, they aren't happening. The concert is supposed to start at seven. It's after six now, and with traffic, probably close to an hour's drive to get there. We wouldn't make it."

"Even if you get there late, you'll still see most of it. Maybe something last-minute came up at work."

Skye dug her fingers into her hair and gripped her scalp. "I knew I shouldn't have gotten involved with a guy so much like our father."

"And what is that supposed to mean?" Rain took a step forward.

"Someone who puts work as his number-one priority." Skye slashed her hand through the air. "I don't want to be an afterthought!"

"Is that really what you think? That dad's first priority is his job?" Rain's voice held incredulity Skye had never heard before.

"What else am I supposed to think? You weren't around, so you didn't see it as much, but every year since Mom died, he's spent more and more hours at the office, and fewer hours at home. By the end of my senior year of high school, I was lucky to see him five minutes before I went to bed. And on college breaks, maybe for one dinner.

"And this summer!" Skye motioned around her. "The whole threatening me to find a job so I can keep my car? Yeah. It's obvious I've only been an obligation to him up until now. A financial leech he had to pay for. Now that he's gotten me through university, he can dedicate the rest of his life to his first love—his job."

Rain's slap came out of nowhere. Skye clasped her cheek where the burning imprint of her sister's hand lingered. Tears welled up in her eyes. How else could she make her sister see the truth?

"I'll just call a ride-share."

"You're a spoiled brat." Rain's words halted Skye's forward momentum. "You think he was working for his own pleasure? That he took on extra projects and missed so much because he liked it?"

"What else am I supposed to think?" Skye's voice was barely audible around the lump in her throat. "It's like when Mom died, I ended up losing two parents instead of just one."

"He did it all for you!" Rain practically shrieked the words. "He wanted to make sure we both had the best chance at life, and he knew he needed money to make that happen. So, he worked and worked and worked to make sure we could achieve all our goals and dreams.

"This summer, he's pushed you so hard because he wants to make sure you can take care of yourself. He knows you have potential, but you need a push—or a *shove*—to use it sometimes. That's why he threatened to take away your stupid convertible. Because he hoped it would motivate you to do what's needed to succeed in life."

"Success in life isn't always measured the same." Skye narrowed her eyes. "And I would've much rather had his time and attention over the years than to be free of student loans and have a car. Those things can be paid off later. Time is gone in an instant."

Rain opened her mouth to say something, but a rap at the front door turned their attention that way. Benjamin stood, a hand shading his eyes as he peered through the glass. Skye had to force her feet to move that way instead of leaving him out there.

"I'm so sorry." He blew in like a half-grown tornado, his hands jerking at the tie around his neck. "I didn't mean to be late, but a friend had a family emergency come up, so I agreed to help, but then I couldn't find witnesses, and the copier was jammed, and ..."

He stopped and ran a finger down her sore cheek. "What happened to you?"

"It doesn't matter." Skye grabbed her bag. "I was about to call a ride-share and head back to Rain's house."

"But the concert—"

"I'm not sure I'm really in a concert mood tonight, Benjamin."

His gaze ran back and forth between her and Rain. "Were you guys fighting?"

Neither of them answered.

"Because of me?" He dropped his hands, his bowtie dangling forlornly.

"My, aren't you full of yourself?" Skye dug her phone out and tapped the app to find a ride.

He snatched her device out of her hand.

Why did people keep doing that? Shouldn't a person be allowed to use her own phone? She wasn't in high school anymore, to have it taken away during class.

"I think we need to talk before you leave." He shoved it in his pocket.

"I don't want to talk right now. I'm sick of talking. It's not like anyone ever listens to me."

"Oh, please." Rain huffed and crossed her arms.

Skye shook a finger at her big sister. "You haven't listened to a word I've said all summer. Or if you did but didn't like what you heard, you pretended I didn't know what I was talking about."

"Or maybe I know more than you think I do, and you just won't give me credit for it." Rain bent over and picked up her box. "But you know what? You think I don't listen? Maybe I'll just stop even trying."

"Real mature!"

"Takes one to know one!" Rain snatched her purse and moved past them. "I'm headed home. You can catch a ride with the guy you think is too much like our father—not a bad thing, by the way. Since we have the best dad in the world."

Skye squeaked a protest, but it was covered up by the clanging of the bells on the door.

"You think I'm like your dad?" Benjamin's voice held a hint of injury.

Skye pinched the bridge of her nose. "More like your job is too much like his."

"Because I stayed late to help a friend?"

Leaning against the counter, she took a deep breath. "It's not just today, Benj."

"Then, explain it to me. What is really so bad about my job?"

"It has the potential to take over your life."

Silence hung heavy in the air between them as her words reverberated through the still shop.

"Explain further." He ground the words out.

"When we did that group date with the funny clothes, you iced over the moment your boss saw you. It was like you shut down your real personality because you were afraid being silly *outside working hours* might lose your job for you. I've seen you deliver work-related things to your uncle at church services, and I'm not comfortable with that. How can you let work filter into God's time? And then, yes, today, you got so wrapped up in work that you couldn't even let me know you might be late."

He took a deep breath, his stance wide. "I fully admit I should've texted. This afternoon was like a series of unfortunate events. That being said, I'm not sorry I agreed to do it."

She wanted to protest again, but it was obvious he was just warming up, because he started to pace in front of her.

"My friend's grandfather's health has been declining rapidly for the last year, and his mom is struggling with all the care he requires. They got an opening at a nursing facility but needed some powers of attorney done before he'd be accepted. It was urgent. And because I helped them with it, they can sleep peacefully tonight, knowing some of their struggles are about to lighten."

Her stomach twisted because it was a good cause, but she wasn't ready to admit it yet.

"As to the other things you brought up, I thought I'd already apologized for my stupidity the night of our dress-up date. And yes. Sometimes, I bring things to Uncle John at the church building. Because I know we'll both be there. And it only takes a second to hand it to him. It's not like we're having a conference or signing things. I don't see the problem with it."

She pinched her lips together.

"I'm sorry you don't think my job is fun enough." He stopped his pacing and faced her again. "But I won't give it up for you. Maybe it's not adventurous or stimulating, but it's fulfilling. I see families leave with peace because they know no matter what happens in life, they're taken care of, and their loved ones will be too. And that's powerful."

"I never asked you to give up your job." The words came out in a mere whisper.

"Not out loud. But you've made it clear from the get-go you didn't like it. Well, Skye, I'm sorry you can't see past your preconceived notions of what you think you want in life." He handed her back her phone. "I hope you find whatever it is you're looking for."

The bells told her he'd gone before she even looked up again.

Why did it feel like everyone important in her life had abandoned her? And why did she have a hunch it was her fault?

19

Stranded. Skye was literally stranded at her sister's shop. And if both people who had left her here were to be believed, she had only herself to blame.

Well, she didn't have to stay here. She shouldered her bag, made sure the door was locked, and headed out on foot, no destination in mind. No way did she want to go back to Rain's house yet. And the concert she'd mostly been looking forward to was no longer an option.

In fact, she could probably also quit thinking about the man who'd offered to take her in the first place. That bridge was going down in flames with every step she took. Good riddance.

She hadn't wanted a relationship anyway. Had told him so at the beginning of the summer. But had he listened? Had he believed her? No. It was *his* fault things had ended this way.

At least, that's what she told herself. Meandering through this part of Boulder at dinnertime made her stomach growl with each aroma meeting her nose. She finally gave in and grabbed a wrap from a café, as well as a coffee. It wasn't something she'd normally get, but it was portable.

"And I don't feel like sitting still right now."

A guy passing shot her a strange look. She'd said that out loud, hadn't she? Oh, well.

Half an hour later, she had no idea where she was. Not anything more exact than the city, anyway. She stopped on a corner to try and remember if she'd ever come this way before.

"Going on a trip?" An older lady stepped up next to her and motioned across the street.

"What?" Skye's gaze followed the finger. Over a bright blue awning, the words *Destination Acquired* scrawled in letters, ending in a paper airplane. A travel agency? She didn't even know brick-and-mortar ones still existed.

She squared her shoulders and gave a nod. "Maybe I will."

"Oh, to be young again." The lady patted Skye's arm and then walked on.

Skye did have some money in savings from working for Rain all summer. Maybe if she got away from here, she could figure out what to do. Without someone always nagging her about growing up or being realistic.

Where would she go? She stepped into the crosswalk and headed toward the little storefront. She'd already done the northeast, Chicago, the Gulf, Atlanta, and New Orleans with Bree and Katie. Not to mention several places in Tennessee. Maybe she'd head west this time. Farther than Colorado, that is.

Instead of the regular bells like Rain had over her door, this one had a welcoming chime. Inside the walls were a perfect sunset orange and covered with posters of various locations. A large desk sat near the back of the area, a bulletin board covered in notes next to it. Near the front were all sorts of brochures and maps, as well as a smaller desk. A few plants near the window, some plastic chairs, and a coffee bar to her left completed the main room.

"I'll be right with you." A friendly voice carried from the back, behind some sort of felt-covered wall.

"No rush." Skye took the opportunity to look around more.

On closer inspection, the various fliers about places were organized by location. Under a sign that simply read *West*, a picture of mountains called Skye's name. She flipped it open and mouthed *Idaho*. She'd never given that state a second thought after memorizing its capital in elementary school.

Washington also had some amazing images on its advertisement covers. Why had she been job-hunting in Missouri all this time? The United States had so much to offer outside her humdrum home state. She could even go to Alaska. Or Hawaii.

"How can I help you today?" A woman—possibly in her sixties—entered from the back. Her silvery hair was short and spiked, and her blue eyes practically sparkled as she beamed a smile. A bracelet covered in charms jangled as she extended her hand to shake Skye's. "I'm Becky."

"Skye. And, honestly, I'm not sure." Skye grinned back. Something about all of this just seemed meant to be.

"Well, this is a travel agency, so you must be looking to go somewhere, right?"

Sighing, Skye's shoulders drooped. "The thought crossed my mind."

"Vacation? Stress relief? Simply wanting to see something new?" One of Becky's brows raised.

"I thought that's what I was doing when I came *here*. But it hasn't worked out quite like I expected."

Becky glanced at her watch. "Know what? It's close enough to closing time; let me flip the sign on the door, and you come back here and talk. Sounds like you need it."

"Oh, no. You shouldn't close early just for—" But Skye's protest was cut off, as Becky had already done it.

The older woman linked arms with Skye and escorted her behind the wall, where a lovely sitting area was set up near a kitchenette. On the other side, doors led to what appeared to be a bathroom and storage closet.

"This is where I like to stay when I'm between customers. These chairs are much cozier than the ones out front. I suppose since it's my place, I could put the cozier ones out there, but it's sort of fun to feel like I'm hiding." She waved toward a red tufted piece. "Sit, sit."

Skye sank down and agreed about it being cozy.

"Tea? Water?"

"No, thank you." Skye curled one leg underneath her, surprised how comfortable she was in the presence of someone she'd just met.

"Okay. Tell me your story. It must be something good for God to have brought you through my door even though you didn't know where you want to go."

God? Skye blinked at the reference. Was coming here tonight a God thing?

"I'm in Boulder this summer because my father told me I had to find a job or lose my car. I've been helping with my sister's wedding planning business while looking for something else."

"Nice car?"

"Red convertible."

Becky gave a curt nod. "I used to have one of those. Now I drive a silver Jaguar."

The edge of Skye's lip twitched, but she schooled it.

"I take it you haven't found anything better than helping your sister?"

Skye shook her head. "Not anything I wanted."

"And what do you want?"

That was the question, wasn't it? Skye released a slow breath. "Something that doesn't chain me to the desk forever. A chance to travel some more. Something I can get excited about and have fun with."

Becky leaned back in her own plaid wingback and tapped a finger to her chin. "How much traveling have you done?"

"A couple of friends and I did several trips together in college. Two spring breaks and some vacations over the summers. New York, Boston, a few places in Tennessee, a quick jaunt down to Florida, Chicago, and earlier this summer we did a crazy road trip from New Orleans across the Gulf Coast and up to Atlanta."

"You've hit quite a few places in the East." Becky nodded. "Got your degree?"

"BA in Marketing."

The older lady's lips pursed in thought. "Ever considered becoming a travel agent?"

Air whooohed from Skye's lungs. Travel agent? The option hadn't even crossed her radar. Was it a possibility?

"I can see from your face, I've shocked you." Becky smiled. "Let me give you the low down, and we'll see what you think afterward."

Skye straightened. "But I don't understand. Why would you do this for me?"

"Before you came in, I was back here praying. You see, I've run this business for several decades now—ever since my George passed away. And I'm still doing okay, but I need some younger blood in here to help me. A person who knows more about technology and some of the more modern ideas. And in the middle of the prayer, you walked in."

Hairs raised on Skye's arms.

"When I heard your story, I wondered if maybe God knew we could help each other out."

Somehow, Skye inhaled deeply enough to say, "I'm listening."

"I can't promise no desk work at all. It's a business, and that comes with most work. But to help people plan a vacation, to make memories and have experiences—that's satisfying enough to overcome the paperwork." Becky held up a finger. "That being said, there are downsides."

Of course, there were.

"Every now and then, you're going to get a call in the middle of the night because someone has lost their directions or their flights were canceled. I had someone call a few weeks ago because she'd lost her passport. Occasionally I even get blamed for bad weather."

"What?"

"I know. It is what it is." Becky shook her head. "But for every one of those stories, I have a dozen good ones."

Skye leaned forward in her chair. "Do you get to travel too?"

"Some. Because I've worked with so many of these resorts and companies for so long, they call me when they have a cancellation that needs filling or give me discounts or free nights to stay. It's not all free, but the discounts make it easier. And it's worth the work required to get it."

Skye nodded. "Would I need more than my college degree?"

"I'm going to be honest. There are courses you can take that would be helpful, but at this point, there's no across-the-board accreditation for each agency. I am registered with the ASTA—the American Society of Travel Agents. They have a great online legal course that helps you be aware of everything you can get sued for and how to cover yourself."

A legal course. The irony wasn't lost on her.

"I'll make you an offer, and you go home and think about it for a week. I don't want to see you back in here before then unless it's to ask questions." Becky rose and grabbed a tablet off the counter.

"If you're willing to take a few online courses, I'll bring you in. I need someone to help with my online presence, and I can train you in other things while you work on that. For the next five years, you can be my employee. Then we can talk about partnership with the option of you taking over full-time when I decide I'm old enough to retire."

Skye took the sheet of paper scribbled with what Becky had just listed. Was this for real?

"We could even talk to your sister about partnering with any destination weddings she might want to plan. I used to have a wedding planner I worked with on those, but she moved out of state, and I haven't found another since. Those can be fun too."

Assuming Rain would ever talk to her again. Would she even let her back in the house when she returned?

"I know it's a lot to think about. After all, travel agents have to be available quite a bit outside of normal working hours. But we have some downtime. And there are perks which outweigh the hard parts—at least in my opinion." Becky waved her hand through the air, setting her charm bracelet clinking and clanging. "Go home and pray about it. That's my best advice. And I'll be praying too."

Skye walked out of the back area in a daze. As she passed Becky's desk, the board full of cards and photos caught her eye. Dozens of pictures of families and couples on vacation filled the area, overlapping and several layers thick. Notes with messages like 'Thanks for helping make our vacation perfect' and 'Thank you so much for finding ways we could afford to do more on our trip. We had the time of our lives!' mixed in the images.

What would it be like to do that? To help someone plan trips like she and Bree and Katie had enjoyed? Bree was the planner. Katie always found historical sites to see. Skye had been more of an in-the-moment girl. Could she take a job that required her to be more like her friends? Or got her blamed for bad weather?

Out on the sidewalk, she requested a ride-share. Part of her wanted to turn around and march back in and agree immediately, but Becky had said she wouldn't accept an answer before a week was up. Besides, Rain needed her for at least one more wedding.

Assuming Rain hadn't thrown all her stuff out on the curb while she wandered Boulder. She slid into the back seat of the sedan and sent up another kind of prayer—that she'd have a place to stay while making the other decision.

***

What had Benjamin done? Had he really just left Skye to fend for herself in finding a ride back to Rain's? Rain, who had obviously hit her sister before he'd walked in. What had that been about?

He turned right and circled the block until he was back in front of Rain's shop. But no lights remained on. Skye was gone. Where, he had no idea.

"That's good. It's fine. It's what I wanted, isn't it?" He tapped his fingers against the steering wheel and pointed his truck toward home. "I was warned. I knew something like this would happen eventually."

Back at his townhouse, he trudged up the stairs, his jacket over his shoulder.

No date. No concert. No dinner. And now no hope of seeing Skye again except across the church building.

His phone dinged, and he quickly dug it from his pocket. Was it Skye?

> Thanks so much for taking care of my Grandpa. Mom was singing as she made dinner tonight, and she hasn't done that in years.

Brody.

In the midst of everything else tonight, he'd almost forgotten what started it all.

> You're more than welcome. So glad I could get it done for you.

And he was glad. All that stuff he'd spouted off to Skye about loving his job wasn't simply anger talking. How could he not love the work?

He just wished he could have the dream job *and* the girl.

Straight through the townhouse, he walked out onto his back patio. Where he froze in shock. Amelia and Clark straightened from perches on his comfy chairs, a fire crackling in front of them.

"Did I know you were coming tonight?" Benjamin raised an eyebrow. Nothing more awkward than walking out to find your newlywed siblings making out on your porch.

"I thought you were going to that concert." Amelia tugged the bottom of her shirt, and Benjamin's cheeks heated.

"It didn't work out. I had something come up at the office that made me too late, and Skye and I ... we aren't really copacetic."

Amelia jumped up and ran over, a frown between her

brows. "Aren't copacetic? Isn't that just a fancy attorney way of saying 'fine'?"

He couldn't handle this right now. "Why are you here again?"

"Your patio is so much nicer than ours. We thought we'd take advantage of the fact you were out tonight and enjoy a picnic dinner here."

"And how did you get into my backyard?"

"Remember how you showed me the trick where your gate doesn't latch all the way? That day I got locked out and needed a place to stay until Dad could get home?"

Benjamin massaged a spot between his eyes that had begun to throb. "Right. Well, please clean up when you leave. And ... next time, could you just ask first?"

"Sorry." Amelia at least had the good grace to look sheepish.

He headed back inside, locking the door behind him. It was one thing for them to take over his back patio. Another entirely to have them waltz into his house.

He popped a frozen pizza into the oven and slumped at the counter. Nothing about this evening had gone the way he wanted it to.

Had Skye found a ride home? Was she safe? Would Rain kick her out for good this time?

"Not my problem." He pushed his phone aside before he could give in to the temptation to check.

20

"We've been talking."

Nothing made Benjamin feel like a teenager called to the principal's office quite like having a meeting with all the senior attorneys start with those words.

He gulped as his uncle cleared his throat and folded his hands together. "Obviously, none of us is getting any younger, though Leon and I think we're not as old as all that yet. However, Frank here is considering retirement in a few years."

Frank Gaines smirked and shook his head at the same time. "Are you trying to make me sound like I'm older than you? Maybe I just have better sense."

This was about Mr. Gaines retiring? Sure, it stung a little that he was the last attorney to know, but he was also the low man on the totem pole in this firm. And it would mean more work for the rest of them, but they could handle the load when the time came. Why the solemn faces when they first sat down?

"Something like that." Leon Marston pushed a page across the table to Benjamin. "This is all subject to change since none

209

of us can see several years into the future. But since Frank gave us a date when he wants to step down, we've talked and thought the time was right to give you something to work toward."

Something to work …

Benjamin drew a deep breath as he accepted the spreadsheet. Goals and expectations for a future partner. He hadn't expected anything like this so soon.

"You know I've always been proud of you." Uncle John grinned. "But you've proven yourself an asset to this firm time and again over the last few years. If you still want to be here in two years and would like to consider taking the role as senior attorney, you're first on our list of people to consider."

Two years.

With a promotion to senior attorney, he could afford something better than his townhouse. Maybe with a yard bigger than a postage stamp. He'd pay off his student loans faster. Could even afford a family.

And there he went down a road he had no right to travel at this juncture. Hadn't the woman he'd thought perfect for him spurned him because of his job just four days ago? If he got promoted to senior attorney, that would mean more work and responsibility. And less chance with Skye Jones.

"There's no pressure to make any decisions today. But we wanted to make you aware of the possibilities. We'll touch base again closer to Frank's retirement date." Marston straightened a stack of papers and gave a brief nod. "But we're all in agreement. We think you'd be a perfect choice."

"Thank you so much." Benjamin rose and shook all their hands, hoping they didn't feel his fingers tremble.

A possible promotion.

It was everything he'd worked for. And yet …

And yet, if he didn't have someone to share it with, what was the point?

He'd seen Skye on Sunday, across the auditorium during worship. She hadn't looked his way a single time. He knew. It had been impossible to take his eyes off her.

She sat beside her sister and brother-in-law, but stiffly, as if all was still rocky between them. His heart ached for the whole situation, but finding a solution was more difficult than not snitching a piece of his mama's fudge at Christmas. In other words, impossible.

Now he had a hope of a more stable future for himself. But even if he were to ask Skye to marry him right now—and if she were to say yes—she wouldn't be happy simply letting him support her. She might not know what kind of job she wanted, but surely she wanted to do more than travel every now and then and have fun. Didn't everyone in the world need a purpose?

Until she figured out what she wanted in life, it wouldn't do either of them any good for him to pursue a relationship with her. Especially since, last he checked, she wasn't thrilled with his job. How could he convince her how amazing his position was? And was going to be?

"Give her up." He ground the words out as he clicked his computer off and gathered a few things to take with him. "Move on."

"Move on?" Marston raised an eyebrow from his doorway just across the hall. "After we just offered you a potential partnership in a few years?"

If the heat in his cheeks was any indicator, Benjamin must be blushing like a tomato. "Not from work, sir."

Marston remained where he was, studying him as if the answer should be plain.

"Just girl trouble." The muttered words escaped Benjamin's

lips before he could help it.

"Come on in." Marston motioned him into his office.

The last thing Benjamin wanted to do was follow his boss, but his feet moved of their own volition. "Don't worry about me, Mr. Marston. I'll be all right."

"I'm sure you will. But I thought I saw something between you and that girl you were with a few weeks ago. What was her name?"

"Skye."

"Right." The older man nodded and sat in one of the chairs in front of the desk, motioning Benjamin to take the other. "Bit of a free spirit, right?"

"You could say that."

"Just like my May." He leaned in as if to share a secret. "She wasn't ready to settle down when we first met, but I convinced her."

Intrigued, Benjamin straightened. "How?"

"Showed her that settling *down* wasn't actually settling. It was simply having someone to go on adventures with. Not to mention having help shouldering the load that comes with life in general." He nodded. "She assumed I'd be a fuddy-duddy, being in law, but then she needed a job, and we needed a receptionist. She worked here for several years and discovered there's more to what I did than just paperwork and legalese."

"That won't work for me. Skye doesn't want a receptionist position—and I'm pretty sure Fern would protest if we tried to replace her."

"Agreed. I'm not getting rid of Fern. But I do recommend you show Skye that there are still adventures after marriage. Or see if one of your clients would be willing to tell her how you helped them. Sometimes hearing it from someone else works better than us saying it."

Would any of that actually work? Skye was more than a

little stubborn. And would she listen to them long enough to hear their story? His first vote would've been Rain before the sisters distanced themselves. Now he wasn't sure she was his best bet.

"Go home and think about it. Pray about it." Marston patted his arm. "Give it to God, and He'll show you what to do."

"Thanks, Mr. Marston." Benjamin rose and shouldered his briefcase. "For hope, if nothing else."

"Sometimes hope is the most powerful tool we have." The older gentleman winked.

But was hope powerful enough to win over a free spirit with lofty dreams?

Okay, God, if this is from you—if I really am supposed to be with this girl You let me grow so attached to—help. Because I have no idea what to do.

"Skye, someone's here to see you." Rain's voice filtered up the stairs.

It wasn't that Skye hadn't heard her sister's voice over the last five days. But it hadn't come often. And definitely not in such a kind tone. Who could possibly be here for her? Please not Benjamin. As much as she'd been tempted to text him over the last few days, she wasn't sure she was ready to see him yet.

Not with him thinking her so hateful and stuck up.

She descended the stairs slowly, spine straight as she braced herself to face the unexpected. Rain had relegated her to mundane tasks upstairs this week. It kept her away from the front desk, which meant farther from Rain. Less likely to have to see each other or talk that way.

It wasn't Benjamin. Her feet froze on the next-to-last step.

Her father stood, arms crossed, feet planted, a scowl holding his jowls in place.

"Autumn Skye, I think it's about time you came home."

Her heart skipped a beat, and she struggled to swallow. "I'm not so sure Missouri is my home anymore."

The words hadn't come out quite as strong as she meant them to, but they also didn't squeak, so she'd count it as a win.

"I suppose you think you're going to stay here and mooch off your sister instead of coming back and mooching off me."

"That's not what I think at all." Her hand gripped the rail, though she wasn't sure if it was to give herself some more support or keep from rushing past him to escape. "I plan to work."

"Work?" He scoffed. "Rain doesn't have much more work for you. And it's time to give your sister back her basement. I agreed to the summer, but it's the beginning of August now. Your time is up."

"And I found a job."

"What?" Rain's voice carried through the curtain to her office space, where obviously, she'd eavesdropped.

Their father glared at her sister and then turned his attention back to Skye. "And what job did you finally decide was good enough for you?"

"I'm going to be a travel agent." She hadn't said the words out loud before. Hadn't fully decided until right that moment.

All week, the pros and cons had swirled in her mind, warring with each other, keeping her from peace. But she kept remembering all those notes and photos from Becky's bulletin board—families so glad she'd helped them plan their trips. And she wanted that. To share her love of travel with others.

"A travel agent?" Her father's brow went up. "And I suppose you think I'm going to pay for whatever training that requires?"

"Not at all. The lady hiring me has included that as part of my pay while I train with her. She's looking for someone younger to help with the online part of her business. And she will be coaching me in the rest. Until I take the few courses she recommended, my marketing degree is exactly what I need."

He rocked back on his heels as if shocked to hear an actual plan come out of her mouth.

"I haven't quite figured out where I'll live yet, but I will." Skye took a deep breath, almost not believing what she was about to say. "And as for transportation, I think I'll get a bike. You can take the car back with you to Missouri."

Rain fell out from behind the curtains and stumbled a few times before righting herself. Their father didn't look much more stable.

"You want me to take your convertible?"

"No. But I think you need to. I need to do this on my own." She gave a little nod. "Was there another reason you were here, or was that it? Because I was almost through sorting those decorations and want to get finished before I leave for the day."

"Stop." Rain's voice had Skye's feet freezing on the next step up.

"Are you going to kick me out?" Skye didn't even turn around. Too much was at stake, and she couldn't face it all head-on like she had a moment before.

"Of course not." Rain huffed and grabbed Skye's hand, tugging her all the way down to the floor. "But there's more that needs to be discussed."

"What?" Skye pulled her wrist free.

"You need to tell Dad what you told me the other day." Rain's voice didn't hold the disbelief and anger from the week before. "Jeremiah helped me see that maybe you were right to feel the way you did about *some* of it."

Rather than comment on how many modifiers that statement had, Skye simply accepted the olive branch it represented. It was a step in the right direction. But, as for the other? Could she actually tell her father how abandoned she'd felt all these years?

His arms were crossed again as he watched both girls having their silent stare off in front of him. How could she open up to him when he looked so grumpy and judgmental?

"Skye thinks you consider her an obligation and responsibility more than a daughter." Rain lifted a brow in challenge as she threw the words out into the still shop.

"What?"

"Rain!"

"Skye, you think I consider you nothing more than a responsibility?" He took a step toward her but stopped. The look on his face was hard to read, but maybe a hint of pain and uncertainty softened the edges of his formerly hard glare.

She pinched the bridge of her nose, squeezed her eyes shut for a second, and prayed for the words needed. "It's what I felt like a lot of the time."

"That's ridiculous! You're my daughter."

"But you spent all that time in the office. Never at home with us. And as soon as I graduated, out came the ultimatum for me to get a job and settle somewhere. It was like you'd gotten me through college, and now you could wash your hands of me."

"No!" His hand sliced through the air. "That's not why I threatened to take away your car. Or any of it."

She waited while he mashed his lips together, his nostrils flaring.

"I wanted to make sure you were okay. That you would be okay if anything were to happen to me where I couldn't take care of you down the road. And I knew the only way to do that was to make sure you found a job. And since you showed no signs of even wanting to look for permanent work, I made that ultimatum. I didn't mean to make you feel unwanted or unloved. Everything I've ever done has been for you girls."

"Working long hours instead of spending time with us? That was supposed to make us feel loved?" Skye fought against the tears choking the back of her throat.

"I wanted to make sure you had everything you could ever want."

"I wanted a daddy." A few tears leaked from her eyes despite the rapid blinking. "That was more important to me than graduating without loans or having the nicest car."

"You love that car. And you'll appreciate not having extra payments as you start this job that probably won't pay much at the beginning."

"I do love that car. But I'd give it back just to have you home more when I was in high school. When Mom died, it felt like I lost both parents at the same time. And then Rain went away to college, and I was basically alone."

"No wonder you don't understand how good a relationship can be." Rain's comment was just above a whisper, but it resonated deep within Skye.

Was it true? Was that why she was so set against finding someone to spend forever with? Because she didn't have enough experience with real relationships?

"Rain, got room for one more guest for a few days?" Their father's voice broke through. "Sounds like we need to talk some things out. Besides, I want to hear more about this job Skye thinks she wants."

He was agreeing to spend time with her—just like that? A tremor ran through her, though from trepidation or elation, she wasn't sure. But something told her that her world was about to be upended in more ways than one.

21

"Believe it or not, I didn't always work long hours." Skye's father sat across from her at the Indian restaurant, slowly turning his glass around and around.

She pinched off a bite of naan and chewed while she listened. It had been so long since he'd had a real conversation with her, she was afraid if she interrupted, he'd freeze up and go back to his normal self. Besides, it took all her willpower to give all her attention to him and not let a bit of it wander back to the first time she ate here—with Benjamin.

"I had just bought the company the year before your mom died. Of course, it was lousy timing. I had to miss so much work while she was sick that we barely made ends meet at work. Then, after ..." He swallowed so hard Skye could see his Adam's apple bob. "After she passed, I guess work was a way to forget for a few hours every day. To push the pain aside and focus on something I actually had some control over.

"I'd come home, guilty for leaving you girls to face it alone, but you seemed better able to comfort each other than I could.

I reasoned it was better that way. That you had what you needed."

Skye shook her head, but he held up a hand, and she clamped her lips shut to listen some more.

"Then, of course, all the expenses of your sister's senior year came at the same time as all the medical bills from your mom's treatments. So, I worked a bit harder each week, knowing if I could get the company back in the black, we'd be okay."

"I guess I never knew about the expenses." She pushed a piece of curry around on her plate.

"And every time I turned around, there were more. Your braces, Rain's college tuition not covered by scholarships, the year the basement flooded, and the roof damage from a close call with a tornado. Cars for each of you, more schooling, Rain's wisdom teeth." He ticked each item off on his fingers. "And I felt like I was inadequate to do it all because I was only one parent. I guess I tried to offset the loss of your mom by making sure you had more than enough fiscally."

Skye let a lungful of air seep slowly through her lips. It made sense, the way he explained it, though she still wished it had been different. But understanding it didn't change anything, did it?

"I didn't realize I was hurting you." His large hand covered hers.

She slowly raised her eyes to meet his gaze. "It's nice to know the logic behind it all. But it doesn't change the fact that I needed *you* more than all the money."

"I can't go back and undo the past. I'd change a lot of things if I could." His usually stoic face sagged as if all the pride and assurance normally there had leaked out. "But I'm hoping we can move forward and make a better future."

She gave a nod. "A better future definitely sounds good."

"And you understand why I gave you the ultimatum this summer? To find a job or lose your car?"

"I do. Though it would've been nicer if you'd simply talked to me and explained it. Or even sat down with me and looked through options." She pushed her plate aside to remove the temptation to continue playing with her leftovers. "It seemed every time you texted to check in on me, you assumed I hadn't tried at all—or that I didn't care what kind of job I got. There's no way I'd want to be an accountant."

A chuckle burst from him, and he ran a hand over his face. "I hoped that threat would be enough to speed up whatever your process was. I knew you had no desire to work there."

"That's rather underhanded, don't you think?" She smirked. "But it also proves my point. You didn't believe I was actively searching."

"Point taken. So why a travel agent?"

She leaned back and crossed her arms over her chest. "The other night, after Rain and I had a fight, I started walking—with no destination in mind. I came across a little travel agency, and it pulled me in. Becky, the lady who owns it, started talking with me. It's been her business for several decades. She'd been praying God would send her someone who could help her, take off some of the workload, and modernize things a bit. I walked in during that prayer."

"You think you're an answer to her prayer?"

"That sounds rather presumptuous, doesn't it?" Skye tilted her head. "And yet, I can't get the idea out of my head. She had a bulletin board full of photos and notes from people she'd helped plan trips for. All grateful for her help.

"And if you think about it, Rain does too. Not trips, but weddings. And another friend told me he can handle the mundaneness of his job because of the satisfaction in knowing he helped someone find peace of mind. I guess every occupation has to have that balance to make it a good one."

"Great points." He leaned forward and looked her in the eye. "But are you sure you can handle the mundaneness you'll probably have too? Or the angry clients who didn't have a perfect experience?"

"I haven't found any job out there without something like that. And at least with this one, there might be an opportunity for travel every now and then. And a chance to share about the places I've visited and loved." She ran a finger over the tilework on the tabletop. "It's worth a try. Nothing else has intrigued me like this opportunity."

"Grab it, then." He nodded and pulled out his wallet to pay their check. "I'll even help you find an apartment and pay the deposit and first month's rent just to show I approve."

Her heart fluttered as if whatever held it down all summer had broken off. "Really?"

"Really." He offered his arm to escort her back out to Pearl Street. "I have a couple of days before I have to go back. Maybe you can practice your new job on me—show me around this town that seems to have taken hold of both my girls."

"That sounds wonderful." And it did. Something she'd never expected at the first of the summer, when all she'd wanted was to get away from her father and his overbearing ways.

"What do you want to do about that car?"

Rosie. The car that had started this whole mess. What did she want to do about it?

"Do I have a choice?" She couldn't meet his gaze. Was too afraid of what she might see there.

"I'm beginning to think you might."

The corners of her lips twitched up. How could they not? Almost everything in her life was looking up all of a sudden. A job opportunity practically landing in her lap. Her father and her on more than friendly terms. Her sister no longer shooting dagger-sharp glares her way. And maybe even the chance to keep her vehicle.

Her fingers itched to call Benjamin and tell him everything that had happened. But the way he'd left her at Rain's shop last week, would he even answer? He thought she didn't approve of him—that there was no chance for a future for them together.

A sudden realization hit her in the chest, and her feet stumbled. She'd judged him just as harshly as she thought her father was judging her. From the very first moment they met, she'd set up a plethora of expectations he'd never be able to meet. And the moment he failed at one, she showed her ire.

"You okay?" Dad squeezed her arm as they walked the rest of the way to his rental car.

"Fine. Just working through a few more things in my head."

"You don't have to figure everything out all at once. Save a few things for next week." He chuckled as he opened her door for her.

Was Rain right earlier? Had Skye set up unrealistic dreams and goals for a relationship because she hadn't had many good experiences with them in her home life? And would she miss out on one of the greatest adventures in life because she was too stubborn to change her mind?

"Dad, will you tell me about you and Mom?"

He looked over as he started the engine. "What about us?"

"Your life together ... your romance. Your marriage. I can't really remember that part very well. I only remember a little about her. And a few things about you before she passed away. But it's hard for me to picture your relationship."

"Your mom was amazing. She had this ability to make anything in life fun, even cleaning the house. She was organized like Rain. But a bit spontaneous like you." His features transformed once again, this time taking on a bit of wistfulness. "I have no idea what she saw in a boring guy like me, but I thanked God every day she said, 'Yes,' when I asked her to marry me."

"And you never found being with one person forever to be boring?" As the words left her mouth, they sounded ridiculous and trite, but there was no taking them back.

"I guess, just like with any job you take, the rest of life follows the same rules. There will be days when bad things happen or it's just the same-old, same-old. But being with the same person through all of it isn't boring. It's comforting. Nice to have that one constant you can count on when everything else is so unstable."

"Comforting like your favorite pair of jeans or shoes." It was like she couldn't help herself. She just kept trying to find something to argue with.

"More like a quilt your grandma made you. Or the Bible when your soul is unsettled." He glanced over at her as he parked behind Rain's house. "Why? Have you found someone you might want to spend the rest of your life with?"

Had she? Or had she blown it when she'd chewed him out for being late to a stupid date?

Benjamin hadn't seen Skye in over a week now—hadn't talked to her in a month. Even if he'd been comfortable putting Mr. Marston's advice into action, he hadn't had a chance. Granted, he hadn't exactly tried to hunt her down, but he figured when he didn't see her Sunday at church services, his opportunity was gone. It was the beginning of September—time for her to be in Missouri again.

This early in the month, the weather was still warm, so he draped his suit coat over the handlebars. He steered his bicycle toward Pearl Street, needing a pick-me-up after a full week of work. Where should he eat this evening? Did anything even sound good?

Maybe he should just go home and heat up something frozen. That was even less appealing. And he was too mature to eat ice cream for dinner.

Skye would, though.

He locked up his bike and started up Pearl Street, dropping a few coins in a pail for the human statue. The silver-painted street performer never ceased to amaze him with his ability to remain motionless for so long. Benjamin definitely couldn't stay so still today, and his feet pounded the cobblestones, headed toward his favorite creamery. The line was out the door, despite the earliness of the evening. He stepped into the queue and studied the chalkboard with the daily flavors.

"I recommend the blueberry lemon."

Afraid to take a breath for fear he'd imagined the voice, he slowly turned to his left. Skye. She was here. With two scoops of ice cream in a cup.

She grabbed his hand and tugged him from the line and over to a bench. And he went despite not having anything to eat yet. Sitting beside her, he still couldn't get his lungs to ease up. Was this a dream?

"Here. Try." Skye held out her spoon, a big bite on the end.

He allowed her to feed him and nodded his agreement about the flavor.

"Ice cream for dinner? Or did you already eat something healthy?" Her eyes sparkled as she grinned at him and took a bite for herself.

"I haven't eaten yet."

Her lips pursed, and she tutted. "Someone's been a bad influence on you."

The ice cream was cold and smooth. The berries tart. He never dreamed this vividly, but she should be gone by now, right?

"You're trying to figure out why I'm here? Or why I'm talking to you?" She offered another spoonful, and he took it automatically.

"Yes." What else could he say? He wanted answers to both questions.

"I live here now." She leaned back, her arm brushing his. "Found a job, of all things."

"A job."

She nodded, her loose braid falling over her shoulder. "At a travel agency."

"Perfect." How had they not thought of such a position before? And how had she found this one? And why did her answer only lead to more questions?

"As for me talking to you ..." She paused while she savored another lick. "I owe you an apology. Or several."

He started to shake his head, but her hand stilled the movement.

"But I was horribly rude. Left you with no way back to your sister's house. Ruined our date."

"And I drove you to all of it. I was upset about so many other things that your tardiness made it all seem worse. The situation with my dad had escalated."

He blinked at her use of the more familiar term instead of *father*, like she'd called him all summer.

"Rain and I were in the middle of a fight over my work situation, as well as my relationship with Dad. I was frustrated that no one seemed to hear what I was saying. And I was terribly confused about what to do with the situation I'd found myself in with you."

"The *situation* with me?" He couldn't ask more than that because she shoved another bite in his mouth.

"Yes. You see, I'd promised myself you were going to be nothing more than one of my FLIRTS. That it would be easy to leave you here when I went back to Missouri at the end of the summer because I didn't want anything deep or meaningful. But you ... were different."

"In a good way, right?" He shifted to face her better.

"Yes. Though I didn't see it at first. I thought you would be boring. Or stuck up, considering your occupation." She held up a hand to keep him from protesting. "I know. I was the one who was stuck up. All my stupid preconceived notions."

"And now?" His fingers reached out of their own volition to tuck a strand of her hair behind her ear. But she didn't complain.

"And now, I miss you."

"Even if I like cauliflower in my mac and cheese?"

Her cute little nose wrinkled. "Maybe except for that."

For the first time in two weeks, a laugh burst from him. "Okay. Agree to disagree on that one. Have you missed me enough to go back to using a nickname?"

"A nickname?"

"You don't even realize it, do you? Several times now, you've shortened my name to Benj."

"Benj." She tilted her head. "Not nearly as bad as Ben or Bennie or Benji, huh?"

He shook his head. "I rather like it."

"Benj. I suppose now you're going to assume I think you're binge-worthy, huh?" Her play on words was quick.

He liked it. "What? You disagree?"

"You put up with my trying to hold you at arm's length. With my stupid rules. My crazy date ideas. You helped me stretch and try new things." She glanced at him from the corner of her eye. "I'd never had a snowball fight in the summer before."

"Give it another month, and we can have a rematch. It has a tendency to snow early here."

"That's going to make the new bicycle I bought seem very cold."

"You bought a bicycle?" Was this the same girl from the beginning of the summer? She looked the same—but not. Because something about her was lighter.

"I did. Figured I had to get around somehow until I earned enough to make a car payment."

"A car payment?" He straightened. "Your dad took your car anyway?"

She shook her head. "I sent it back with him until I can afford it."

"Wait. He was here?"

"Yes." She scraped the last bite of ice cream from the container and spooned it into his mouth. "We worked through some things, but that's another story for another day."

"Wow."

"What?" Her big blue eyes blinked.

"You've changed so much."

"I'm still me." She held up the paper cup. "Eating ice cream for dinner. Though that didn't fill me up nearly as much as I planned."

"I hope you're still you. Because you're who I fell in love with." Would those words scare her off? She'd been adamant she wanted nothing to do with such sentiments at the beginning of the summer. But after this conversation, he had more hope than ever before.

"Love me enough to take me for some real food?" She jumped up and gave his hand another tug.

"I can be convinced."

"Good. Because I could never love a man who wouldn't feed me every now and then." There was the flirty smile he'd been missing.

"How about a lawyer with a possible promotion to senior attorney in a few years?"

"Funny story about that." She linked her arm through his. "Turns out I need to take a few courses on the legal side of being a travel agent. So, I guess maybe I'll be able to hold a conversation with you after that."

"As if you couldn't hold your own before?" He poked her side, making her squeal. "And you didn't answer the question."

She stopped, faced him, and took both his hands in hers. "Benjamin Smith, will you be my plus one at my friend Bree's wedding next month?"

"I'd be honored, but—"

She lifted up on tiptoes and pressed her lips to his in a quick kiss. "Good. Because I want them to meet the man I love and am so proud of."

It took him a minute to blink out of the haze she'd just put him in, and by then, she'd gone several feet down the sidewalk. As he raced to catch up with her, his mouth stretched wide in a probably ridiculous-looking grin. But he didn't care. Nor did he care that he was facing a future of lots of crazy moments like that.

It was worth it.

EPILOGUE

October
Bree

Finally.

After several months of more marriage counseling, as well as Nathan receiving additional counseling to deal with his issues, Bree would finally walk down the aisle and become Mrs. Hart. When their family had suggested they wait after getting back together, it had been one of the hardest decisions they'd made. But she couldn't deny how much more ready she felt now.

He'd pulled her aside after the rehearsal the night before and prayed with her. Something he'd never been bold enough to do before. They'd both grown—together and in themselves.

"You about ready?" Her dad stuck his head in the doorway and gave a half-smile. Suspicious moisture pooled in his eyes.

"More than ready." She turned so he could get the full picture.

"You look beautiful, Bree Baby." He straightened and cleared his throat. "Your mother and I are so proud of you."

"Thanks, Daddy." She stepped into her sandals and gathered her flowers. "We couldn't have made it this far without your and Mama's support. That's for sure."

He carefully wrapped her up in a hug, patting her back awkwardly, as if afraid to mess up her dress or veil. "We only wanted you to have the best possible chance of a forever love."

"We're both committing to it. And Nathan isn't as afraid anymore. He knows he's not his father." She grabbed her father's hands and squeezed.

"You're going to do great. You've got your teaching job, and he's got his accounting business. And you're only two hours from us. But it's still going to be hard for me to say I'm giving you away."

"Not giving away. Just gaining a son to go with your two daughters."

He shook his head and swallowed hard. "Doesn't mean everything won't be different now. You've been my responsibility your whole life. And now you're going to be his."

"I've had you and Mama to show me how a marriage should look." She winked. "Besides, I promise to come home every Christmas and snuggle beside you on the couch while we watch *It's a Wonderful Life*. Who else is willing to sit there for so long and pretend they don't see you crying every year?"

He gave a playful scowl. "Maybe I won't miss you that much after all."

The laughter helped ease the bittersweetness of the moment. He was right. This was the beginning of something new between them. But she was okay with that. Even though their relationship would be different, he'd still be her Daddy. And she was ready to finally be a wife.

"Bree, we're about to start." Katie poked her head in the door and smiled.

"We're coming."

Everything was perfect, despite being four months later than she'd first planned. October colors were prettier than the hues she'd originally chosen, anyway. And she and Nathan had received back almost every gift they'd returned after their breakup. Their home would be well-stocked and filled with love.

As her bridesmaids walked out to the music, she couldn't help wanting to rush out there with them. Who decided a bride should wait until after everyone else went in? She wanted to be up there now!

The flower girl toddled her way out. Several titters of laughter filtered back through the closed doors. What had the preschooler done? She'd find out later. Almost her turn.

"Last chance. Sure you want to do this?" Her father's teasing whisper sounded in her ear as they stepped up to the doorway.

"One hundred percent."

"Let's get you in there, then."

The doors opened, and the audience rose as one to watch the bride. But she didn't pay a lick of attention to who had come today. Her eyes zeroed in on the front, where Nathan stood, hands clasped in front of him, a look of trepidation in his eyes.

Stage Fright.

She kept eye contact with him all the way down. He never looked away, but he didn't smile. As her father placed Bree's hands in Nathan's, his frigid fingers trembled around hers. Poor introverted guy.

One corner of his lip lifted for a mere second as she gave

him a squeeze but then disappeared again. It was enough. She had a grip on him now and wasn't letting go ever again.

"Dearly beloved." The ceremony started.

She didn't need to hear it word for word today. She'd caught the important parts last night during rehearsal. As long as she repeated the right phrases, they'd be married at the end. That was all that mattered.

When the minister asked Nathan to repeat his vows, he did, his voice shaking and quieter than normal. But the words were loud enough for her to hear.

It was almost Bree's turn, and she willed him to relax just a bit more. The longer he stared at her, not letting his eyes look anywhere else, the warmer his fingers grew and the less stiffly he stood. He even smiled at a few things the minister mentioned. Her heart slowed down.

His gaze darted toward the audience and then back to her again. But, she knew he could rest easy. Because this was the only time she'd require him to stand in front of a whole room full of people like this. One marriage for life. That's all she wanted—and today, they were promising each other that's what they'd have.

Katie

Katie swatted at Camden's hand as he stole a bite of her chocolate cake. "Eat your own!"

"I mean, the white cake is good, but that chocolate ..." He reached toward her again, but she pulled her plate farther back.

"Uh-oh. Is he giving you trouble? Because I was just bragging about him being here earlier, and now you're hitting him?" Bree stood beside them, her beaded gown swishing as it brushed against their chairs.

"He was trying to steal a bite of my cake." Katie pointed to her plate. "You'd do the same thing."

"Oh. I want a bite. I didn't get to try that one." Bree leaned over and borrowed Katie's fork to take a bite for herself. "Mmm."

"Seriously?"

"This may be the most I get to eat until we get to our hotel tonight." Bree pouted, but in a playful way.

Katie leaned back where she could see both Bree and Nathan better without craning her neck. "What's the consensus? Where did you decide to go on your honeymoon?"

"He won't tell me. You'd think after the debacle over the summer, he would've learned his lesson." Bree pouted in Nathan's direction, but he just grinned. "I'm still hoping for NYC, though."

Holding a hand up where Bree couldn't see his lips, Nathan mouthed, 'It's NYC.'

Giggles burst from Katie. Bree would be thrilled.

"What did he say?" Bree looked back and forth between them.

"Have fun wherever you end up. I can't wait to hear all about it." Katie squeezed Bree's hands before they moved on to talk to other guests.

Camden ran a finger up the bottom of her foot, shooting more than just a ticklish sensation through her legs. She gasped and started to pull her feet off his lap, but he held on. "Sorry. Couldn't resist."

"What's the scoop?" Skye plopped down in the chair next to Katie. "Are you two officially dating, after all?"

Camden raised an eyebrow, and Katie hesitated. What did that look mean? They'd been dating five months and were even talking about marriage someday. Had she missed something?

"We're officially a couple." Camden shot her a concerned look after she didn't answer. "A couple of what is yet to be determined."

"Nice." Skye passed over a piece of paper. "I guess you'll be wanting this, then."

Katie leaned forward and saw the caricature Skye had commissioned of just her and Camden that day in New Orleans. In the middle of each of their eyes were little hearts instead of the normal white space. Their faces were cartoonish but discernable. She traced the edge of the card-stock and smiled. That day she'd been livid, but now it was a treasure.

"You keep it." Camden pushed it to her. "Looks like it makes you happy."

"You don't want it?" Katie studied his face, but he wasn't giving anything away.

"Tell you what. I'll hang it on my wall when it's your wall too." His words sent shivers through her heart. The meaning behind it all was serious and full of promise.

"Whoa." Skye pushed back from the table. "You guys move too fast for me."

He twined his fingers through Katie's. "Besides, I don't need another souvenir from that trip. I got the best."

"I thought I got the best." She grinned. "Speaking of trips—my mom wants you to come with me for Thanksgiving in a few weeks. Unless you have other plans."

"As long as you don't bring back another souvenir from Alabama." Humor sparkled behind his eyes.

"Like I could find another in as good condition!" She tugged her hands free and crossed her arms, not really upset with him, but wanting to let him squirm a bit. "Besides, the last one I acquired was one of a kind and nonreturnable."

"You don't regret picking me up?"

She tried to stop her smile from forming but couldn't. "Never."

"Good. I look forward to meeting your parents. Just let me know the exact dates so I can ask off."

She didn't have a chance to reply because Nathan called for everyone's attention. "All the single ladies, Bree wants to throw her flowers at you. Please come line up over here."

Katie groaned. "I hate this part."

"They're waving at you. I don't think you can get out of it." Camden patted her foot.

"Maybe I'll just push Skye in front of me and let her catch it." Katie didn't bother grabbing her shoes to hobble across the linoleum floor and stand with the other unmarried girls.

"Okay, ladies. Here it comes." Bree glanced over her shoulder and winked right at Katie.

She's going to throw it at me.

The tightly bound roses flew into the air as if in slow motion, the ribbons fluttering behind like a kite tail on a summer day. Gasps echoed through the room as the bundle collided with the ceiling fan, spinning off in a direction away from where Katie stood. The tension in her chest released until a pair of hands shoved her from behind, knocking her back into the line of fire.

Squeals and laughter reverberated around her as she lifted her head from the floor. The bouquet lay in her hands, only slightly worse for wear. She didn't even want to think about how her dress had fared from that ungraceful tumble.

"Katie! Katie, you caught it!" Bree's squeals of excitement almost made it worth the bruises sure to appear on her knees later tonight.

"Yay." Skye's voice came from the direction of the pusher, and Katie narrowed her eyes at the blonde.

"You pushed me." Katie shook the roses at Skye.

Skye held both hands in front of her. "Me? Why would I do something like that?"

"Need help getting up?" Camden gently grasped her elbows and pulled her back to her feet. "I must say, I've never seen anyone go after it like that. I thought you were going to let someone else catch it."

"Fate, or something like it, intervened." Katie spit the words out around clenched teeth.

"This means you're next in line to get married, huh?" Camden pointed to the flowers.

"Supposedly."

"They may be waiting for a while." His grin eased the frustration inside her.

She smiled back. "Maybe."

Or maybe not.

Skye

"Did you seriously push her?" Benjamin poked Skye as she joined him on the outskirts of the room.

"Push?" She blew out a pshaw. "I prefer to call it a helpful nudge in the direction she wanted to go anyway."

"She didn't look like she agreed."

"She'll get over it." Skye grinned. "I do think I win the biggest surprise of today, though."

"Why's that?" He bumped his shoulder into hers.

"I don't think anyone expected me to bring you. Or for you to exist at all."

"Because I'm more permanent than anyone else you've dated?"

"Because you're more than just a passing fad. They used to joke that I had a different date every week during college."

"Did you?"

"Sure you want to know?"

"You know everything about you interests me." He ran a finger down her cheek.

She rested her head on his shoulder. "I probably did. Sometimes more than one per week."

"Just because you hadn't met me yet."

"Exactly." She gave him a grin. "Among other things."

"How did it feel standing up as a bridesmaid today?" He nudged her. "Too close to being a bride?"

As much as she'd like to say yes, she couldn't lie to him. "Honestly it wasn't that bad. Much easier than expected, despite these awful shoes."

"Think you might be willing to stand up on a stage during a wedding again?" His question was leading, and she knew exactly what he was asking. But that was pushing it too far today.

"I have a feeling I'll be standing up for Katie's wedding in the near future. She and Camden look rather cozy, don't they?" She wagged her eyebrows. "Good thing I grabbed that caricature when we picked up my car."

She and Benjamin had flown into St. Louis because Dad signed her convertible over as a surprise for her birthday last month. They'd driven it down to the wedding in Nashville and would take it back to Colorado on Monday. Though Benjamin said she was going to slide all over the roads this winter in her crazy little thing.

He wove his fingers through hers. "You know that's not what I was asking."

"I do know that's not what you were asking, but I'm not sure I can handle the other thought yet." She couldn't meet his eyes, too afraid she might disappoint him.

He leaned close, his mouth right next to her ear. "Maybe someday, when you're ready, we can talk about other options."

"Other options?" She leaned back to see his face.

"I hear there's this thing called eloping." His stage whisper was over-the-top and set her to giggling.

"Rain would never forgive me."

"It's not her choice. You're a different person than she is and can do things your own way."

"But would you be okay with that?" She quickly added, "If this thing between us ever came to a point where we wanted to talk about forever, of course."

"I don't know if you remember this or not, but I was in two different weddings this summer. I saw everything required and how much craziness ensued. I'd be more than happy to skip all that hullabaloo—especially if it gets you to agree to go through with it in the first place."

"Every day, I learn something new about you, Benjamin Smith." She straightened his lapel.

"And you thought I was going to be boring." He smirked.

"I'm not ready for anything like that yet." She wagged a finger his way.

"I know. But I'm patient. And I'll be here when you are."

For the first time in her life, having something permanent sounded amazing. He might not need as much patience as he thought. Because the more she got to know him—as he helped her with learning her new business, as he surprised her with repeat date nights he knew she'd enjoyed or something different, as he traveled with her to be in her friend's wedding—the more she liked the idea of spending the rest of her life with him.

Her definition of adventure had morphed completely since the beginning of the summer. And her definition wasn't the only thing that had changed—she had.

But wasn't that the sign of a good adventure?

The ~~End~~ Beginning

AUTHOR'S NOTE

Dear Readers,

This series was so much fun to write. I hope you've enjoyed taking a few trips with my girls as much as I did.

Skye was my wild card. When I wrote the first book, I honestly wasn't sure how to redeem her—because let's be honest. In the first story, she isn't as loveable as the others are. Now that you understand her reasoning and history more, I hope you love her as much as I do. She's got her own way of doing things, for sure.

Boulder, Colorado, is absolutely gorgeous in the summer. My family was blessed to all get together there the summer after my daughter was born. We hiked, explored Pearl Street and the Celestial Seasonings factory (seriously, the best-smelling place in the world!), and enjoyed time nestled in the Rocky Mountains. And yes, we did throw snowballs at each other in June! I tried to include a lot of our fun experiences here so you could visit it through my characters' eyes. And if you get the chance, go! It's beautiful.

With this being my last book in the series, I didn't want to leave you hanging on what happened with Katie and Bree. Hence, that last chapter, where you get a peek into everyone's head. I hope you enjoyed seeing all the happy endings and that it gave you some closure on all their stories.

Thanks for riding along on this journey. As always, if you enjoyed the story, please let others know and leave a review. This helps authors much more than you can imagine.

Until the next story, God bless you wherever He takes you!

Love,
Amy

DISCUSSION QUESTIONS

1. Skye is afraid to get serious because she thinks in extremes: either serious or fun. Why is this such an unhealthy way to look at life? Do Benjamin and Rain do a good job of showing her otherwise?

2. Working for a wedding planner is a bit ironic to Skye since she doesn't have any desire to get married. Do you think working for such a business would help or hurt in convincing someone marriage is a good thing?

3. Benjamin loves his job and is very excited about future possibilities with his firm. But he also wants to maintain a balance between work and the rest of his life. Is he always able to do this? Could he have done better?

4. When Skye first arrived in Colorado, she was less than impressed. But Colorado has a lot to offer, from hiking to quaint shopping spots, to miles and miles of hills and mountains. Just like life, sometimes we don't give things/people/places

enough of a chance when we first see them. Have you ever had to learn a similar lesson the way Skye did?

5. When Rain mentions the possibility of future children, Skye immediately wants to be the best aunt possible. Though it means showing more responsibility and stability than she has, it's worth it for nieces and nephews. Have you ever had something enter your life that inspired you to do better? Do you think Skye will eventually prove herself trustworthy enough to be added to the guardian list in Rain's will?

6. Benjamin chooses to stay late and help a friend who needs assistance for his grandfather sooner rather than later. This makes Benjamin late for a date with Skye. Was the peace given to Benjamin's friend worth the trouble it caused in his relationship?

7. Rain doesn't see her father the same way Skye does because she remembers him more before their mom died. Do you think one girl sees more truth than the other? Or do you think their father changed that much when his wife passed away, making him different to each daughter?

8. Skye wants a job she can consider fun because she never wants to end up like her father has—a workaholic and prioritizing work above all else. Even though there are jobs out there more fun than others, every business has its downsides, as Becky and Rain both point out. Do you think she'll be happy in the occupation she's chosen?

9. Skye's father doesn't realize how much he's ostracized himself from her. In the end, as they

both lay out their reasons and thoughts, they reach a better understanding, though there is still some work to be done before their relationship is mended all the way. Have you ever had to have a heart-to-heart with a family member and found out neither of you saw the whole picture?

10. In the end, all the girls ended up with happy endings, though Katie and Bree were a bit shocked when Skye brought a serious date to Bree's wedding. Do you think each girl got just the lesson she needed on her road trip? Can you imagine what kinds of trips they might take in the future now that Skye is going to be a travel agent?

ABOUT THE AUTHOR

Amy R Anguish grew up a preacher's kid, and in spite of having lived in seven different states that are all south of the Mason Dixon line, she is not a football fan. Currently, she resides in Tennessee with her husband, daughter, and son, and usually a bossy cat or two. Amy has an English degree from Freed-Hardeman University that she intends to use to glorify God, and she wants her stories to show that while Christians face real struggles, it can still work out for good.

Follow her at http://abitofanguish.weebly.com or http://www.facebook.com/amyanguishauthor

Or https://twitter.com/amy_r_anguish

Learn more about her books at https://www.pinterest.com/msguish/my-books/

And check out the YouTube channel she does with two other authors, Once Upon a Page (https://www.youtube.com/channel/UCEiu-jq-KE-VMIjbtmGLbJA)

MORE ROADTRIP ROMANCE ...

Destination: ~~Fun~~ Romance

~~Roadtrip Romance~~ Book One

It's not every day you bring a boyfriend back as a souvenir.

Katie Wilhite is ready to settle into her new job as a librarian now that college is through, but friends Bree and Skye want one more girls' trip, and when Bree insists this is her bachelorette fling, Katie agrees. What she didn't agree to was allowing fun and flighty Skye to dictate the itinerary or for her anxiety to kick in harder than ever ... right in front of a cute guy.

Camden Malone had no idea when he agreed to be the voice of reason on his cousin Ryan's vacation that the trip wouldn't stay in New Orleans as planned. But when Ryan plots with Skye so that the guys can tag along with the girls all week, he isn't nearly as upset as he should be. Not with Katie's fiery temper and flashing eyes intriguing him more by the minute.

Can Katie relax enough to trust Camden and a possible future, or will she continue to push him away as only a vacation fling? And can Camden move past a rocky history of his own to be able to jump into a better future? For a trip that was supposed to be all about fun, there's a lot of romance going around.

Get your copy here:

https://scrivenings.link/destinationromance

Roadtrip for ~~***One***~~ ***Two***

Roadtrip Romance—Book Two

Recovering from heartbreak is hard when

the ex-fiancé tags along ...

Dallas wasn't in the plans when Bree Henley set out to use the nonrefundable honeymoon tickets from her canceled wedding. Nor was running into ex-fiancé Nathan Hart. But their mutual friends and the weather have other ideas. A hurricane cancels their cruise and Bree decides to turn the disaster into a roadtrip for one, never imagining Nathan would object.

Nathan is furious when he uncovers the plot to get him back with Bree. But he can't just let her go roaming around the big city of Dallas alone. Though he knows calling off their wedding was the right thing to do, he still cares for Bree. And before he knows what hits him, he's volunteered to tag along. Suddenly, it's a trip for two.

Spending the week together might remind them of why they fell in love. But is it enough to overcome the obstacles standing in the way of "til death do us part"?

Get your copy here:

https://scrivenings.link/roadtripfortwo

ALSO BY AMY R. ANGUISH

Love Delivered

A novella collection, including "Romance at Register Five"

by Amy R. Anguish

Mack McDonald isn't happy about the Grocerease app coming to his grocery store. But he's committed to the sixty-day trial period, and braces himself to lose money. Kaitlyn Daniels loves how the Grocerease app helps her make ends meet so she can assist her mom, the reason she moved to small Sassafras, AR. Mack and Kaitlyn struggle to overcome differing opinions on the perks of the app. But if they don't, it could keep them from something even better.

Get your copy here:

https://scrivenings.link/lovedelivered

No Place Like Home

Can love secure Adrian's wandering heart?

Roots are overrated, at least to someone like Adrian Stewart, preacher's kid, who has never lived anywhere longer than six years. That's why her job with MidUSLogIn Inc., is so perfect for her—lots of travel, and staying nowhere long enough to have it feel like home. But when work takes her to Memphis, closer to her family for the first time in years and in the same small office as Grayson Roberts, she starts to question her job, her lack of home, and even her memories of her rocky past with the church.

Gray is intrigued by Adrian from the moment he sees her, and he's determined to get to the bottom of why this girl, who loves old movies and hums when she works, won't go to church with him. As they grow closer, he wants more too, but how can he convince her to stay in Memphis when she doesn't believe in home—or God? Can he use his own broken past to break through hers?

Get your copy here:

https://scrivenings.link/noplacelikehome

Saving Grace

Michelle Wilson's one goal in life was to become a top journalist at the local paper back in her hometown of Cedar Springs, AR. But on the way to bringing that dream to reality, a life-changing wreck interrupts Michelle's plans and adds an orphaned baby into the mix. Now, she has tough decisions ahead—did God put her in that accident to save baby Grace? And if so, why is it so hard to convince everyone else she should be the baby's new mommy?

Greg Marshall has been Michelle's best friend his whole life. He's thrilled she's moving back home, but not so sure about her sudden desire to be a single mom. His feelings for her have grown through the years, but she's never seemed to notice. Can he help Michelle with the adoption and grow their relationship at the same time?

Get your copy here:

https://scrivenings.link/savinggrace

Faith and Hope

Get your copy here:

https://scrivenings.link/faithandhope

An Unexpected Legacy

Get your copy here:

https://scrivenings.link/anunexpectedlegacy

Faith Moves Mountains by Jenny Carlisle

Book Two in the Crossroads Series

John Kennedy (John K.) Billings has spent his whole life living up to his hero inspired name. Now, back from a traumatic incident in the military, he finds himself running from the fact that he is only human, with real-life struggles to overcome.

Faith Caldwell feels free to pursue her own dreams now that her family's regularly scheduled rodeo has ended. After helping care for her cancer-stricken mother she is determined to bring big city medical expertise to small-town Arkansas. While trying to prove she can fulfill her dream on her own, a new admirer seems determined to pull her down.

Both enjoy the idea of seeing more of the world, but find their hearts are still tied to the mountains of Arkansas, and the people who live there.

Can these lifelong neighbors help each other face their weaknesses while following God's plan for their lives?

Get your copy here:

https://scrivenings.link/faithmovesmountains

Forever Home by Hope Toler Dougherty

Book Three in the Forever Series

With a fulfilling job and a home of her own, former foster child, Merritt Hastings, relishes her stable, respectable life. Dreaming for more is a sure way for heartache. When a contested will turns her world upside down, she must revaluate what's important to her, what's worth fighting for, and what's worth sacrificing.

Patience has never been Sam Daniels' strong suit with his history of acting quickly and asking questions later, and he's ready for changes in his life...now. Too bad the plans for acquiring a radio station didn't include a contract. Now he's out of a job, out of a radio station, and out of prospects.

While his life is in flux, at least he can help Merritt steady hers, or will he rush in and overstep ...again?

Will the sparks flying between these two opposites lead to a happily-ever-after or heartbreak for both?

Get your copy here:

https://scrivenings.link/foreverhome

Stay up-to-date on your favorite books and authors with our free e-newsletters.

ScriveningsPress.com